# YORK NOTES

*General Editors:* Professor A.N. Jeffares (*University of Stirling*) & Professor Suheil Bushrui (*American University of Beirut*)

## E. M. Forster

# HOWARDS END

*Notes by Caroline MacDonogh*

BA (DUBLIN) MAITRISE D'ANGLAIS (SORBONNE)
*Junior Lecturer, University of Caen*

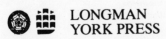

**LONGMAN
YORK PRESS**

YORK PRESS
Immeuble Esseily, Place Riad Solh, Beirut.

LONGMAN GROUP LIMITED
Longman House,
Burnt Mill,
Harlow,
Essex

First published 1984
ISBN 0 582 79243 6
Printed in Hong Kong by
Wilture Printing Co Ltd.

# Contents

# Part 1

# Introduction

EDWARD MORGAN FORSTER was born on 1 January 1879. Shortly after his birth his father died of tuberculosis, and so the child was brought up exclusively by his mother. Her family name was Whichelo; her father had been a drawing master at grammar schools in Stockwell, London. The family was modest and socially obscure, and Lily, their third daughter, was lucky to find a benefactress in Marianne Thornton, whose family were bankers and leading members of the Clapham sect, champions of the anti-slavery movement. Not only was this to give her a complete social and family background, but she was also to meet her husband through the Thorntons: Edward Forster, a rector's son, was a nephew of Marianne Thornton, who went to Charterhouse school and then Trinity College, Cambridge, before taking up architecture. Because of his early death he could not influence his son's childhood, and Forster was always closer to his mother, never showing any curiosity about, or attachment to, his father.

His mother was to dominate him throughout her life, and he rarely lived apart from her until she died. Two and a half years after Edward Forster's death, Lily and her son moved from London to Rooksnest, Stevenage, Hertfordshire, the house which was to inspire Howards End. Forster's life there was paradisial, spent mostly out of doors, playing with the son of the neighbouring farmer, Frankie Franklyn, whom he continued to visit later in life. Another friend was Ansell, one of the garden boys, who gave his name to a character in Forster's second novel, *The Longest Journey* (1907), and inspired a short story entitled 'Ansell'.

Forster was a precocious child, teaching himself to read at the age of four and writing short stories at the age of five. During these early years he was surrounded by what he himself termed a 'haze of elderly ladies', some of whom were to feature in various ways in his works. One of whom he was particularly fond was Louisa Whichelo, his maternal grandmother, a witty and lively woman who was the model for Mrs Honeychurch in his third novel, *A Room with a View* (1908). Another was 'Maimie', the widow of his benefactress's nephew, Inglis Synott, whose remarriage after her husband's death contributed to the plot of his first novel, *Where Angels Fear to Tread* (1905).

Looking back on these years later as a schoolboy, Forster wrote a nostalgic description of Rooksnest, and the similarity between the house of *Howards End* and these notes of his is very striking. Forster's first experience of school was a rude break with this life; at the age of eleven he was sent to Kent House, a preparatory school at Eastbourne in Sussex. Sensitive and rather marked by his mother's mollycoddling, he was an ideal bully's prey. Although unhappy, he managed to work hard at his studies, and in his Christmas examinations in 1892 was top of his form in Classics, French and Scripture. By now the lease of Rooksnest had expired and the Forsters moved to Tonbridge in Kent, where Forster became a day boy at the public school. The following two years were probably the unhappiest in his life. The moral attitudes and discipline did not suit his artistic temperament for he was far from being an ideal English schoolboy. During these years, however, he was cultivating a knowledge of the classics that was to give a firm foundation to his writing, and eventually he even earned popularity and respect because of his intelligent and witty conversation. None the less, his miseries at Tonbridge left a lasting impression on him, and he recapitulates this episode of his life through Sawston school in *The Longest Journey*.

Cambridge was to exert an influence too, but in a very different way, by bringing him into contact with a whole intellectual universe that would confirm his inherent outlook on many things. One of the basic attitudes, reflected in *Howards End*, is an innate belief in the survival of the cultural heritage of man, and a complementary awareness of the growing menace to civilisation. This resulted in a disdain for the up-and-coming Tory business class, and a tendency to see scholars and civil servants as the true leaders of society. At the time the prestige of the professions had increased, but Forster did not share in the general approval of them; indeed he seized many a literary opportunity to show up doctors and clergymen. The Cambridge 'truth' of the day, inspired by the philosopher G.E. Moore's (1873–1958) *Principia Ethica* (which appeared in restated form in his *Ethics*, 1916), can be summed up as an aesthetic faith in the essential role of human intercourse and the cult of the beautiful as fundamental to social progress. Moore was the chief luminary of the 'Apostles', the Cambridge Conversation Society, to which Forster was elected in 1901.

There was an enormous gap between this life and the suburbia around the home where he now lived with his mother in Tunbridge Wells. It was there he came into contact with that respectable society of afternoon teas, of tennis clubs, which emerges from the social comedy in his work, in particular in the suburbia of 'Sawston' portrayed in *Where Angels Fear to Tread*.

Forster graduated in history and classics in 1901, and went off for a year's travel through Italy and Austria with his mother. He was able to afford this thanks to the legacy left to him by Marianne Thornton. The life he later wrote of her expresses his gratitude, and in its final words actually recognises that she made his 'career as a writer possible'. In Italy he was to visit San Gimignano, the model for the town of 'Monteriano' in *Where Angels Fear to Tread*. He wrote a short story there, 'The Story of a Panic', and it would seem that during this sojourn he realised that he would most probably become a writer.

On his return to England he took up a post as lecturer at the Working Men's College in Bloomsbury, where many Cambridge dons and graduates taught. This college was founded in 1854, with the aim of helping to alleviate the cultural deprivation of the under-privileged. John Ruskin (1819–1900) and Dante Gabriel Rossetti (1828–82), among others, had lectured there, and the link with Cambridge was very close, with an annual gathering at Cambridge for the students of the college. In Leonard Bast's attempts at self-improvement in *Howards End* Forster expresses his slightly ironical view of something in which he had been closely involved, especially as he taught there for twenty years or more. In 1904 he also lectured on Italian art and history for the Cambridge Local Lectures Board, and contributed to liberal journalism through the *Independent Review*. In that year he moved to another suburban home, this time in Weybridge.

In 1905 he had experience of Germany as tutor to the children of Elisabeth, Countess von Arnim (née Mary A. Beauchamp, 1866–1941), author of *Elisabeth and her German Garden* (1898), and it was there, at Nassenheide in Pomerania, that he received the proofs of his first novel: in October 1905 *Where Angels Fear to Tread* was published. It was successful, its sales encouraged by favourable reviews. In this novel, Forster shows the mediocrity of English suburbia in contrast with Italian spontaneity and colour; yet his love for the English countryside, as shown in *Howards End*, was beginning to grow, and he began to cover the landscape on long walking tours. The year 1906 marks the beginning of the friendship which orientated him towards India when he became tutor to Syed Ross Masood.

During the next two years he published two more novels: *The Longest Journey* (1907) and *A Room with a View* (1908), and both got very good reviews. *The Longest Journey* is his most directly personal work, Rickie Elliot being very close to himself. *A Room with a View* springs from his experiences in 1901, when he lived in a *pensione* in Florence.

A first sketch of *Howards End* appears in Forster's diary in 1908, where he mentions that *Howards End* is to have a 'wider canvas' than his other novels; during the following year social outings, a dinner party, casual conversations or acquaintanceships, all contributed further observations which were incorporated into his writing of *Howards End*. He worked on it all the summer of 1909, and on its publication in

1910 the press almost unanimously referred to the event as Forster's 'arrival', and the term 'Forsterian' came into use. It marked a turning point in his life, as he became a celebrity.

During this time he was moving from a peripheral relationship to the Bloomsbury Circle,* and was becoming increasingly involved in their activities. A landmark of this association is Roger Fry's (1866–1934) portrait of Forster, painted in 1911. Also in 1911 Forster published *The Celestial Omnibus*, a collection of short stories; these were written at various times over the past years, and accompanied the writing of his novels. They are really preparatory to the novels, a more whimsical and less subtle revelation of the 'unseen'.

In October 1912 Forster left for India, and this journey greatly influenced his future writing, which culminated in *A Passage to India* (1924). In 1913, on his return to England, Forster's friendship with Edward Carpenter (1844–1929) and a visit to the home Carpenter shared with a group of Uranians,† all revering the same notions, confirmed Forster's confidence in his homosexual life. In 1914, he finished *Maurice* (1971), a novel based on his affair with H.O. Meredith, a fellow student at Cambridge, but he decided it was not to be published until after his death.

At the outbreak of the 1914–18 war Forster became cataloguer for the National Gallery in London, leaving this position in 1915 to work for the Red Cross in Egypt until 1919. A book materialised from this experience, *Alexandria, a History and a Guide* (1922). In 1921 he returned to India, and during his stay accumulated material for *A Passage to India* which was already under way before his departure. Its publication, in 1924, was a resounding success. Mrs Moore, in this novel, like her predecessor Ruth Wilcox, is a gentle and unassuming person who incarnates the presence of the unseen throughout the work.

This was to be Forster's last novel, and it is difficult to know why he never returned to this form. When asked he would simply reply: 'I have nothing more to say.' In 1927 he gave the Clark lectures at Cambridge, where he spoke about the novel, and these lectures were published under the title *Aspects of the Novel* (1927). In 1924 he had moved to a country home, West Hackhurst, at Abinger, near Dorking, the lease having been left to him by an aunt. He participated increasingly in various activities, constantly writing letters, articles and petitions, reacting against Nazism and Stalinism with vigour. He also took part in many congresses and sat on committees. In 1934 and in 1942, he was

---

* This was a group which began to meet about 1906 and which included, among others, Vanessa and Clive Bell, Roger Fry, Lytton Strachey, and Virginia and Leonard Woolf. Their aesthetic philosophy was largely inspired by G.E. Moore (see p.6).
† Uranians revered the same notions of comradeship, suggested by the naming of their community after Uranism, a form of male homosexuality.

President of the National Council for Civil Liberties. In 1934 he published a life of his Cambridge friend, Goldsworthy Lowes Dickinson (1862–1932), an affectionate and interesting study for what it conveys of the Cambridge atmosphere. His last visit to India took place in 1945; it was arranged through the PEN association of writers, but he was disillusioned with many changes that had occurred.

His mother died in 1945 at the age of ninety, after years of close companionship, a relationship in which Forster complained but kept constantly in touch when away. He was elected an Honorary Fellow of King's College, Cambridge, and was to spend the rest of his life there in residence, although for the first seven years he did not live in his rooms but with friends in Cambridge, the Wilkinsons. In 1947 and 1949 he went to lecture in the United States, at Harvard and the Academy of Arts and Letters. In 1949 he began working on the libretto of Benjamin Britten's opera *Billy Budd*. *Two Cheers for Democracy*, a collection of essays, appeared in 1951, and *The Hill of Devi*, about the princely state he stayed in in India, Dewas Senior, in 1953. In 1945 came *Marianne Thornton*, the biography of his benefactress.

In these late years Forster suffered extremely bad health, but had a most surprising resilience; he saw many of his friends die before him. His close friends, the Buckinghams, took him to their home whenever he fell seriously ill, and it was there, at Coventry, that he eventually died on 7 June 1970.

## A note on the text

*Howards End* appeared on 18 October, 1910; it was published by Edward Arnold, London. The book was acclaimed by A. Marshall in *The Daily Mail* as 'The Season's Great Novel', and turned E.M. Forster into a renowned literary figure overnight. A paperback edition of *Howards End* is published by Penguin Books, Harmondsworth, 1941; latest reprint, 1981.

# Part 2

# Summaries
*of* HOWARDS END

## A general summary

The novel opens with a description of Howards End, a house in Hertfordshire, and this is given through letters addressed by Helen Schlegel
to her sister, Margaret Schlegel, who has stayed at home at Wickham
Place in London to look after their brother, Tibby, who is sick with
hay fever. A move from this first objective, exterior description is
made by the conclusion of the novel, where the house has become the
centre of the Schlegels' existence. Helen's first two letters are followed
by a brief note stating that she and Paul, the younger son of the family
she is staying with, the Wilcoxes, have fallen in love. Back in London,
her sister is considerably upset by the news, and their Aunt Juley, who
is staying at Wickham Place, goes by train to see what the situation is.
Margaret, back from seeing off her aunt, finds a telegram from Helen,
saying that all is over between herself and Paul.

Aunt Juley is picked up at the station by the elder Wilcox son, Charles,
who is rather unpleasant. Helen is in tears; the mother, Ruth Wilcox,
calm and dignified, seems aware of what has been happening. Helen and
Aunt Juley return to London. Helen explains her disillusionment with
Paul, who had yielded to family pressure and disowned his feelings
very quickly.

Helen and Margaret resume their cultural activities. One of these is
going to concerts, and, after listening to a performance of Beethoven's
Fifth Symphony, Helen is extremely moved, leaving before the concert
is over. Her sister has got into conversation with a young man they do
not know, and Helen absent-mindedly takes his umbrella off with her.
Leonard Bast accompanies Margaret home to get his umbrella; he
leaves hurriedly, taking their card with him. He goes back to a depress-
ing suburban flat, where his companion, a rather blowzy woman, joins
him for supper. He tries to read Ruskin's *Stones of Venice* (1851–3),
but his companion, Jacky, does not make it easy.

The Schlegels discover that the Wilcox family have taken a flat just
opposite them. Helen is not very affected by this; she is off to Germany,
having been invited there by her cousin, Frieda Mosebach. When she
has left, Margaret writes a note to Mrs Wilcox declining any further
acquaintance. She later regrets this, and on visiting Ruth Wilcox, finds
her charming. They become friends; Ruth Wilcox comes to lunch with

Margaret and her intellectual friends; they go Christmas shopping together. On this occasion Margaret declines Ruth Wilcox's invitation to go directly to visit Howards End, to which Ruth is obviously deeply attached. But then Margaret changes her mind and joins Ruth at the station; when they are ready to leave they are interrupted by the arrival of Evie Wilcox and her father, Henry; their motoring tour has been cut short by an accident.

Mrs Wilcox dies after an illness. The funeral over, her family are shocked to hear that she has left Howards End to Margaret Schlegel in a note written at the nursing-home. After debating the matter, Henry and Charles decide to burn the note (Paul, the younger son, is in Africa) and they do so in the presence of Evie and Dolly, Charles's wife. Margaret, unaware of Ruth's request, is grateful to receive her silver vinaigrette as a present from Henry Wilcox. She welcomes back her sister, who has turned down a marriage proposal from a German friend of her cousin's.

Two years pass and the Schlegels' brother is now at Oxford; Margaret is concerned for his future, and worried about their having to leave Wickham Place as the lease is soon to expire. A visitor calls, looking for her lost husband. Next day, Leonard Bast calls, explaining that the mysterious lady was Jacky (now his wife), looking for him because he had not come home that night; inspired by his reading, he had taken an all-night walk in the country. Jacky had seized on the Schlegels' card as providing a possible address to which he might have gone. The girls go out to dinner at a Chelsea discussion society, and during their debate they cite Leonard as an example of the under-privileged. Afterwards, Helen and Margaret go along the Chelsea Embankment, and they run into Henry Wilcox. He tells them that the insurance firm where Leonard works as a clerk is going to crash. They invite Leonard to tea to warn him; Henry and Evie arrive, and Henry is shocked to see them receive Leonard.

Margaret is increasingly concerned about having to find somewhere else to live. She lunches with Henry and Evie and her fiancé. Henry offers to help Margaret. She and Helen go on their annual summer holiday to Aunt Juley, at Swanage. Margaret gets a letter from Henry, offering to rent them his London house. When she visits it he proposes to her. Helen, when Margaret returns to Swanage and tells her, is upset, and against the marriage. But Margaret accepts, and when Henry comes down to see them they hear by letter that Leonard has given up his old job for a less well-paid one. Henry says Leonard's old job was a good one; the company is no longer in danger. Helen is furious, and Margaret realises that Helen hates Henry. Margaret visits Howards End, and loves it. She goes to Henry's home in Shropshire for Evie's wedding. After the reception, Helen arrives with Leonard and Jacky;

they are impoverished, Leonard having lost his job. Jacky recognises Henry, her lover of ten years before. Helen and the Basts sleep in the local hotel. Margaret, after a short time of reflection, forgives Henry.

Helen visits Tibby; she is leaving for Germany and wants to give five thousand pounds as compensation to Leonard, who refuses it. Wickham Place is emptied and the furniture goes to Howards End for storage. Margaret is married, and lives in London for the winter; she and her husband are building a new house. She goes to Howards End to find that Miss Avery, the neighbour, has unpacked and arranged their furniture in the house. She decides to get it stored in London, but has no time as Aunt Juley is seriously ill with pneumonia. Helen is called, but replies that she will only be able to stay a very short time, and when Aunt Juley recovers Helen just leaves her address with their bank in London, which refuses to give it to Margaret. Realising that Helen is avoiding her, Margaret becomes anxious. On Henry's advice she arranged for Helen to see the furniture, as she wishes, at Howards End, and they 'ambush' her there. She thus discovers at Howards End a pregnant Helen; she protects her from the menfolk. Helen wants to stay at Howards End for a night; Henry refuses and Margaret is shocked at his lack of understanding. Margaret and Helen nevertheless sleep the night at Howards End, and Margaret learns that the father of Helen's child is Leonard.

Leonard, since the night in Shropshire with Helen, has been full of remorse. He eventually tries to find the Schlegels, and arrives on the morning of the night they have slept at Howards End. Charles, who has just arrived at the house, attacks him; he succumbs to heart failure. Charles gets three years' imprisonment and Henry, distressed, falls back on Margaret. Helen, Margaret, Henry and Helen's son all live together at Howards End. Henry decides that Howards End will be Margaret's; Ruth Wilcox's wish is fulfilled.

## Detailed summaries

### Chapter I

Through an epistolary approach we are introduced to the house of the title. The first of these letters, all from Helen Schlegel to her sister Margaret, is written on Tuesday, and describes the house and surroundings; a wych-elm is given particular mention. We learn that Tibby, the girls' brother, has hay fever in London, which has kept Margaret at home there with him. The inhabitants of Howards End, the Wilcoxes, are presented: Mrs Wilcox in an image of flowers and hay, the others— the daughter Evie, the son Charles and her husband—all described humorously, at various activities. The second letter, dated Friday, accentuates Mrs Wilcox's unselfishness and the masculine charm of Mr Wilcox. The last letter, dated Sunday, says that Helen and Paul, the younger son, are in love.

COMMENTARY: We are given a full view of Howards End and the well-to-do Wilcoxes in their conventional country life. Mrs Wilcox contrasts with the prevalent atmosphere. Helen's humour emerges, as does her femininity; there is dramatic irony in her encounter with Mr Wilcox, as her attitude will later change radically. The last letter's announcement is typical of Forster's taste for surprise, and links this chapter to the next by suspense.

NOTES AND GLOSSARY:

**a-tissue:** an onomatopoeic word, conveying the sound of sneezing, emphasising the motifs of hay and hay fever that run through the novel

**Kings of Mercia:** Mercia was one of the Anglo-Saxon kingdoms. The Mercians spread into Hertfordshire in the seventh century

---

## Chapter II

---

At Wickham Place, London, at the Schlegels' house, Margaret and her Aunt Juley receive the news. We learn how the Schlegels and the Wilcoxes met, on holiday in Germany. Margaret defends her sister against interference, but, anxious, accepts Aunt Juley's offer to go and see about the 'engagement'. Tibby is too ill to be left. Margaret accompanies Aunt Juley to King's Cross railway station. A telegram awaits Margaret's return: all is over between Helen and Paul.

COMMENTARY: Aunt Juley with her observations gives us a standpoint from which to view the Schlegels and the Wilcoxes. She suggests the liberal, Schlegel tradition and the possible philistinism of the Wilcoxes. The city, a recurrent theme, is seen to be linked to the countryside by the various railway stations. Forster makes a humorous personal intrusion, then launches the plot with a second surprise.

---

## Chapter III

---

Aunt Juley's thoughts in the train portray the family history. Her sister had died when Tibby was born, when Helen was five and Margaret thirteen. Their father died five years later. Her nieces live on the income from investments. Arriving at Hilton station she finds Charles, the elder Wilcox son, but presumes he is the younger, Paul. Trying to discuss matters in the car she is embarrassed to discover that he is Charles; none the less, she reacts indignantly to his annoyance on learning of Helen's and Paul's engagement. At Howards End, Helen is trying to explain the situation when Mrs Wilcox appears. Calm and obviously aware of the affair, she disperses everybody.

COMMENTARY: The opening is stylistically original, combining social and individual history in a character's thoughts. Charles's aggressiveness comes over forcefully in his manner and his driving. The survival of the past emerges in the person of Mrs Wilcox.

NOTES AND GLOSSARY:

**Deceased Wife's Sister Bill:** this bill, allowing a man to marry his sister-in-law, was finally passed in 1907, after sixty-five years' debate

## Chapter IV

Helen and her aunt return to London. Helen's experience is discussed, and she and Margaret opt for the 'inner' life over the 'outer', the latter leading only to 'panic and emptiness'. Their idealism is explained by their Germanic origins, and by their childhood which was spent amidst adult intellectual discussion. Helen's more attractive physique is contrasted with Margaret's solidity.

COMMENTARY: Helen's disillusionment gives rise to a strong reaction; masculine strength turned out to be weakness. Harmony reigns as the girls cultivate friendships, attend intellectual gatherings. None the less, Helen's experience was unique, warns Forster, a romantic encounter never to be repeated; he also warns the reader of Helen's vulnerability, arising from her impulsive nature.

NOTES AND GLOSSARY:

**Forward Policy in Tibet:** Imperialist policy, and, in the case of Tibet, a reference to the Younghusband expedition of 1904, sent to forestall Russian influence. It led to a convention with Tibet in the same year

**Esterház:** court of the famous Hungarian nobles, the Esterhazy family, especially associated with the patronage of composers, Franz Joseph Haydn (1732–1809) in particular

**Weimar:** famous as a literary centre in the eighteenth and early nineteenth century

## Chapter V

Queen's Hall: the Schlegels are at a concert, with their cousin, Fräulein Mosebach, her young man and Aunt Juley. Margaret chats to a young stranger; Helen, moved by Beethoven's Fifth Symphony, leaves, accidentally taking the stranger's umbrella. The young man, anxious to get it back, accompanies Margaret to Wickham Place after the concert; he listens helplessly to Margaret's cultured conversation on the way. On arrival, Helen's vivacious manner scares him away. The Schlegels' witty chat, about the feminine atmosphere of their home, ends the chapter.

COMMENTARY: These thoughts, reflected by music, afford a further example of Forster's originality. Two extremes are Tibby's knowledgeable concentration, Helen's interior voyage to 'panic and emptiness'. Notice the recurrent symbols of the 'goblins' in the drum passage, parallel to the young man's umbrella. Margaret's talk with him emphasises an enviable insouciance procured by education, as also does the final conversational scene.

NOTES AND GLOSSARY:

**Queen's Hall:** a concert hall at Langham Place, London, privately built. It was destroyed during the Second World War

**Monet:** Claude Monet (1840–1926), French impressionist painter

**Debussy:** Claude Debussy (1862–1918), French composer

**Miss Corelli:** pseudonym of Mary Mackay (1864–1924), the daughter of Charles Mackay, a Scottish poet. A popular novelist, she wrote, under the name Marie Corelli, *Thelma* (1887) and *The Sorrows of Satan* (1895), among other novels

**Cairngorm pin:** Scottish Highland costume jewellery of a smoky yellow variety of quartz

## Chapter VI

After leaving the Schlegels Leonard Bast returns to his suburban flat. The atmosphere is bleak. He breaks the frame of a photograph; it is of a woman called Jacky. While he is reading Ruskin's *Stones of Venice*, she appears. Their conversation consists of dull, repetitive exchanges. He gets up to make a meagre supper, then plays Grieg on the piano. She goes to bed, interrupting him as he tries to read. We learn that she is thirty-three; he has promised to marry her when he is twenty-one.

COMMENTARY: You should notice here Forster's art as a social realist, and, in the portrait of Jacky, his gift for caricature. He introduces the theme of 'gentility', created by Democracy to which he granted two cheers in a later essay where he discussed the effort of the under-privileged to improve themselves. Jacky's mental dullness is expressed by her poor vocabulary. A wide cultural gap is portrayed by the altera-tion of the sentence from Ruskin, which Leonard adapts to his own life: 'luminousness' becomes 'obscurity' just as daily life intervenes in Leonard's spiritual aspirations. Forster realistically asserts the contri-bution of sound finance to an artist's life.

NOTES AND GLOSSARY:

| | |
|---|---|
| **Ruskin:** | John Ruskin (1819–1900) was one of England's greatest masters of prose. *The Stones of Venice* contributed greatly to his reputation as an art critic |
| **Watts:** | George Watts (1817–1904), English historical and portrait painter. He is known for his portraits of Tennyson, Swinburne, Gladstone and others |

## Chapter VII

The next morning Aunt Juley announces a surprising piece of news: the Wilcoxes have moved into a flat opposite the Schlegels. She and Mar-garet, arranging flowers together, worry about Helen, who arrives and blushes on being told the news. Margaret advocates risk and spontan-eity in life, saying that it is impossible to plan or to protect oneself in such situations, but also adds that people like themselves, living on so much invested money a year, are rendered more invulnerable than others. They go to find a domestic servant at the registry office. On their return Helen announces she is off to Stettin, invited by her cousin Frieda. She swears indifference to the Wilcox family.

COMMENTARY: This chapter features one of Forster's characteristic traits in narrative: coincidence, a device which allows him here to maintain the Schlegel-Wilcox link. Margaret's definition of their money as a protective island is fundamental in the novel, asserting that interaction between money and the spiritual life which runs throughout the narrative. Her aphoristic remarks about the poor express Forster's own awareness of the financial basis to individual freedom, and refer us back to Chapter VI.

## Chapter VIII

It is now a fortnight later; Mrs Wilcox has called, which annoys Mar-garet, as Helen is happily packing for Germany, the past forgotten. It is a dreary November evening; Frieda and Helen have left. Margaret writes a note to Mrs Wilcox asking for their acquaintance to end. A reply the next morning makes her ashamed. Paul has gone to Africa. She goes to see Mrs Wilcox and finds her in bed; Evie and her father are on a motoring tour. She learns of Charles's marriage, the main reason for their stay in London. Mrs Wilcox shows her a framed photograph of Dolly (Charles's wife), and Margaret accidentally breaks the glass. She hears of Mrs Wilcox's attachment to Howards End, and of the pigs' teeth in the wych-elm to cure toothache. They part friends.

COMMENTARY: Light and shadow suggest death in the opening and closing images of Mrs Wilcox. There is a bizarre use of coincidence when Margaret, like Leonard in Chapter VI, breaks the glass of a photograph frame and cuts herself. Mrs Wilcox's identity merges with Howards End, and the biographical associations with Forster are enriched by the wych-elm.

NOTES AND GLOSSARY:

**native hue of resolution ... thought:** a quotation from Shakespeare's (1564–1616) *Hamlet* : 'And thus the native hue of resolution/ Is sicklied o'er with the pale cast of thought' (Act III, Scene I)

## Chapter IX

At a luncheon party at Margaret's given in honour of Mrs Wilcox, there is clever, lively conversation with references, in particular, to Germany, art, music and women's suffrage. In this talk Mrs Wilcox plays little part; she stands out as rather unintellectual, and lonely. In saying goodbye Margaret is apologetic, a little revolted by her friends' cultured banter, protesting, however, that they and she too have something of Mrs Wilcox's calm wisdom. She returns to the dining-room where her friends have decided that Mrs Wilcox is uninteresting.

COMMENTARY: Forster achieves a fine interplay of mentalities at this gathering, no doubt with personal experience of fashionable intellectual coteries in mind. As elsewhere in the novel Mrs Wilcox's personality ultimately pervades and prevails. Despite her experience as a cultured hostess, Margaret loses confidence in her kind of conversation. The juxtaposition of the motor-car and the flower concluding Chapter III recurs here, clever conversation being a further social counterpart of the motor-car in its encounter with Mrs Wilcox's personality.

NOTES AND GLOSSARY:

**Rothenstein:** Sir William Rothenstein (1872–1945), painter, lithographer and art critic

| | |
|---|---|
| **Böcklin:** | Arnold Böcklin (1827–1901), Swiss painter of allegorical landscapes |
| **Leader:** | Benjamin Leader (1831–1923), English landscape painter, especially of Welsh mountain scenes |
| **MacDowell:** | Edward MacDowell (1861–1908), American pianist and composer, particularly renowned for his orchestral tone-poems |

## Chapter X

Mrs Wilcox takes Margaret Christmas shopping in foggy London; between helping Mrs Wilcox, who seems tired and indecisive, Margaret confides in her that the lease of Wickham Place will expire in two or three years, and flats are to be erected in its place. On their return Mrs Wilcox proposed to bring Margaret down to Howards End, but she declines and Mrs Wilcox is offended; they continue their way home in silence. At lunch with Tibby, Margaret changes her mind and resolves to go over to the Wilcox flat, but Mrs Wilcox has already left. She follows her to King's Cross. They meet there, but the trip is postponed as Evie and Mr Wilcox arrive, an accident having shortened their tour.

COMMENTARY: The city of London is shown in another light: Margaret and Mrs Wilcox shop in a background of cold, bustling commerce. Forster's image is precise and brittle; the air is like 'cold pennies'. Margaret's reactions are his, evoking the survival of human values amidst the anonymous crowd and lost significance of traditions. Notice how the trip to Howards End springs from the 'imagination'; its failure means the triumph of the prosaic.

NOTES AND GLOSSARY:

| | |
|---|---|
| **Backfisch:** | (*German*) a baked fish, but metaphorically an awkward girl |

## Chapter XI

Mrs Wilcox's funeral is over; afterwards we see the graveyard, set in the surrounding countryside. The following morning, the Wilcox family are at breakfast at Howards End, Mr Wilcox upstairs, Evie, Dolly and Charles downstairs. Evie brings up the post to her father, who has been meditating on his wife's past goodness; he hasn't eaten anything. Charles goes out to complain to the chauffeur, saying that his car has been driven unbeknownst to him. Dolly comes out to tell him that his father wants him. Mrs Wilcox, in a note sent on by the nursing-home matron, has left Howards End to Margaret. Horrified, the men have an urgent discussion; then they throw the note in the fire.

Charles suspects Margaret, but his father considers her honest and helpful, as unaware of Mrs Wilcox's impending death as they were themselves.

COMMENTARY: This chapter provides a shock for the reader; Forster prefers not to narrate, but springs the unexpected quality of life itself on us. Notice how the men handle the affair of the will; this is an excellent piece of social comedy

NOTES AND GLOSSARY:

**Ulysses:** in Greek mythology, when his ship was about to pass the island of the Sirens, creatures who could draw men to destruction with their singing, Ulysses filled the ears of his men with wax

## Chapter XII

Margaret does not hear of Mrs Wilcox's bequest. After her death she feels close to her and to them, appreciating their realistic attitude to life. Consequently she writes a warning to Helen, not to overconcern herself with personal emotions. Helen returns in January, and she, Margaret and Tibby recount each others' news. Helen has turned down a proposal in Germany; Tibby has been up to try for a scholarship to Oxford; Margaret was asked in a letter by Charles if his mother had wanted her to have anything; his father later sent her a silver vinaigrette after she had replied that Mrs Wilcox had wanted to give her a Christmas present. Margaret, recapitulating the past months, realises the chaotic element in life, and its romantic essence.

COMMENTARY: Notice the opening sea image which runs throughout the whole work. Survival is linked with Mrs Wilcox, and implies hope, even after death. An indication of Margaret's closeness to Forster is her pursuit of unity and balance. Refer back to Chapter IV to see how similar detailed imagery weaves the texture of the plot together: telegrams, anger, grit, sloppiness. Margaret's reasonable thoughts conclude on a complementary awareness of the unpredictable beauty of existence.

## Chapter XIII

Easter, two years later: Margaret begins to apprehend the expiry of their lease. She discusses Tibby's future with him; he is down from Oxford on vacation, and she is trying to instil in him a sense of purpose, citing the Wilcoxes as an example. Helen is preparing a speech downstairs on political economy; she suddenly appears, explaining that a woman has called, looking for her husband. By her amusing imitations of the visitor, we realise that this woman was not of the same class as the Schlegels. Her visit makes Margaret unpleasantly aware of their approaching instability.

COMMENTARY: The expiry of the lease seems to threaten the solidity of the 'island' on which the Schlegels live; Margaret appears as the stable centre of the family. Helen's humorous dialogue is a delightful moment of comedy, and the reference to the umbrella provides an ironic detail when we learn later who the visitor was. The chapter ends with the goblin footfall, expressing the same disharmony as in Chapter V.

NOTES AND GLOSSARY:

**Mr Vyse:**      a character in Forster's novel *A Room with a View*
**Mr Pembroke:**      a character in Forster's novel *The Longest Journey*

## Chapter XIV

Next day Leonard Bast arrives, to explain his wife's visit. The girls do not recognise him immediately, but become enthusiastic when he elucidates the circumstances. We learn he is a clerk for the Porphyrion Fire Insurance Company. Inspired by his reading of various works, he had decided to take an all-night walk in the countryside. Jacky, taking the Schlegels' card from his first visit (it had been an object of jealous curiosity for her), had gone to the Schlegels on the following afternoon to find Leonard; he, in the meantime, had gone back to their suburban flat. The girls listen to this, fascinated, but have to go off to a dinner engagement. Leonard returns on foot, exalted by their appreciation.

COMMENTARY: Forster evokes in Leonard a creature exiled from nature, from his rural origins, by modern civilisation. Literature is defined as a signpost, leading ultimately to something greater than itself; compare Forster's observation in Chapter XXXI on the inhabitants of the demolished Wickham Place as being people who did not mistake culture for an end in itself. The easy dismissal by the girls of literary examples is ironical, as for Leonard literature and culture in general constitute an insurmountable difference between himself and the Schlegels.

## Chapter XV

The dinner-party is made up exclusively of ladies, and they debate the subject 'How ought I to dispose of my money'? Bast is quoted as an example of the under-privileged. Margaret asserts that independent thoughts are the result of independent means, that money is the warp of civilisation. They leave, accompany a girl to Battersea Bridge Station, then turn on to the Chelsea Embankment. In their conversation they mention Mrs Wilcox; Mr Wilcox, near-by on a bench, hears them. He tells them Bast's insurance company is going to collapse; he is prosperous and content with life. After he has left, the girls decide to tell Bast about his company.

COMMENTARY: Social history contemporary with the novel appears in this evocation of a women's society, showing Forster's preoccupation with the feminine mind, already expressed by the principal roles of Helen and Margaret. Margaret's realism concerning the dependence of the imaginative faculties on finance reflects one of the main aspects of 'Only connect . . .', the opening motto chosen by Forster as an introduction to his novel. The coincidence of meeting Mr Wilcox jolts the theoretical debate into material existence.

NOTES AND GLOSSARY:

**Territorials:**     a voluntary military force on a territorial basis, formed in 1908

## Chapter XVI

Leonard comes to tea the following Saturday; he resents the ladies' interference in his everyday life. He would prefer to discuss literature, but they ask about his salary and prospects. He finally manages to introduce books into the conversation but is interrupted by the arrival of Mr Wilcox and Evie with puppies she has bred. An argument develops as Leonard wishes to leave, declaring that the afternoon has been a failure. Margaret defends their sincere interest; Mr Wilcox proposes to help but Helen sees Leonard out. Margaret explains the circumstances, but the Wilcoxes insist on considering Leonard as typical of his class. Helen, annoyed with Mr Wilcox, wants to help Leonard. Mr Wilcox, driving away, says to Evie that the girls are so unpractical, they need protection.

COMMENTARY: Relationships evolve; Leonard's with the Schlegels becomes more complicated, and this confrontation between the Schlegels and Mr Wilcox establishes new associations between them. Helen's former admiration of Mr Wilcox finally turns to strong dislike. Mr Wilcox's mild appreciation of Margaret is deepening into attraction. It is only Margaret, solidly occupied by her cause, who betrays no change of feeling; she is none the less aware of playing a role between the two men, aware that Henry Wilcox is 'titillated'.

## Chapter XVII

Margaret is increasingly anxious over the imminent move; she resolves to concentrate on house-hunting, but accepts an invitation from Evie

Wilcox to lunch at Simpson's (see Notes and Glossary below). Ill at ease with Evie, who has her fiancé, Percy Cahill, with her, Margaret is delighted that Mr Wilcox has joined them. The discussion turns to her move, and she appeals to Mr Wilcox for help. Afterwards, Margaret declines to accompany them to the Hippodrome and leaves them, encouraged to think that the invitation to lunch was really Mr Wilcox's. She later takes him to a health food restaurant, with Tibby as chaperone. Next day the Schlegels leave for their annual summer holiday with Aunt Juley in Swanage.

COMMENTARY: Wickham Place, a little like Howards End, has come to be emblematic of permanence, especially now that the Schlegels have to leave it. It is a survival in the midst of nomadic modernism where houses no longer have a past. Even furniture ownership does not compensate or convey the same continuance.

The conversational exchanges at table, particularly at the moment of discussing auras, interspersed with the choice of cheeses, are skilful both as linguistic expressions of two different personalities and as well contrived examples of light conversation veiling ultimate psychological realities.

NOTES AND GLOSSARY:

| | |
|---|---|
| **Simpson's:** | a restaurant famous for its traditional English food, in the Strand, London |
| **Parson Adams:** | a character in Henry Fielding's (1707–54) novel *Joseph Andrews* (1742) |
| **Tom Jones:** | hero of Henry Fielding's novel *Tom Jones* (1749) |

## Chapter XVIII

The action takes place at Aunt Juley's: Margaret receives a letter from Mr Wilcox, asking her to come up and see his London house in Ducie Street if she is interested in becoming a yearly tenant. Margaret suspects he may make a proposal of marriage, but gradually dismisses this notion. She finds Mr Wilcox waiting at Waterloo railway station, a bit strange in himself; as they drive to the house she realises she enjoys his company. While visiting the house, he proposes, and Margaret is taken aback at having been right. His proposal is most unemotional. She leaves him immediately, saying that she will reply by letter, and goes to Wickham Place for the night. There, she decides to wait and talk to Helen; she respects his lack of romanticism, swearing never to expect any of him. She senses Ruth Wilcox as a presence, but not an embittered or resentful one.

COMMENTARY: Margaret's thoughts run as a motif through this chapter. The psychology of her reaction is interesting: having dismissed her premonition, she is then overcome by its realisation. The term 'central radiance' is an apt description for a character whose role is as a centre from which the novel's principal ideas radiate. Her self-awareness regarding her own feelings, her lucid objectivity, prepare the way for her eventual compromise and reconcilement with outer reality.

NOTES AND GLOSSARY:

**Cruickshank:** George Cruickshank (1792–1878), the artist, caricaturist and illustrator

**Gillray:** James Gillray (1757–1815), the artist, caricaturist and engraver

## Chapter XIX

The Schlegel's cousin Frieda is on the hills above Swanage with Aunt Juley and Helen, who feels close to Frieda's Germanic idealism. Tibby is driving Margaret up from the station. Mystery surrounds Margaret's 'No' when they ask her about Ducie Street. She whispers about the proposal to Helen, who is very upset and weeps. To explain this Helen recalls her earlier reflections on panic and emptiness. Margaret exposes her own realistic attitude: she is going into it with her eyes open; his people are the sort who have civilised life. Helen feels that such a marriage is incomplete.

COMMENTARY: The chapter opens, and also closes, with a view of England; there has, however, been a change in the view: Margaret's words introduce an additional element which is Forster's own question concerning the contribution of civilisation. Such passages justify *Howards End* 's reputation as a song to England, and Forster states the deep association between his imagination and his country at the end of the first paragraph. The closing passage adds to this vision, aiming to reconcile nature and man, and as elsewhere it is Margaret who voices this aim. The last question reverberates in the reader's mind, opening on an ambiguous unity of inner and outer forces. One very melodramatic appeal to sentimentality is in Helen's stance, weeping on the hill.

## Chapter XX

Realistically facing the absence of romance in Henry, Margaret accepts the proposal. The next day Henry arrives in Swanage with the ring, staying at a near-by hotel. That evening he dines at Aunt Juley's; Margaret laughs at herself in her first love-scene: a stroll along the Parade. He is keen to discuss future money settlements, and their future home. Margaret suggests Howards End, but a tenant, Hamar Bryce, has it on three years' lease since the preceding March. Margaret converses with vivacity and humour, contrasting with his heavy insistence on serious, practical subjects. He, feeling strong and protective, sees her back, kisses her suddenly in the garden, and rushes away. This upsets her; she thinks of Helen and Paul.

COMMENTARY: Margaret's love appears to be a confirmation of friendship, rather than opening on to the novelty of passion. Henry's lack of emotional involvement is obvious in his indifference to her conversation; simultaneously he shows a male protectiveness. The analysis of man-woman relationships is subtle; underneath Margaret survives the impact of his personality by her resilient self-awareness that will later prove to be the solid foundation of their partnership. His sexual advance is a counterpart to his emotional poverty in its abrupt crudeness. Margaret's sudden remembrance of Helen and Paul implies Henry's repression of their passion.

## Chapter XXI

Charles has been angry with Dolly for having introduced his sister to her uncle, Percy Cahill; if Evie wasn't to marry, Mr Wilcox would not have felt lonely, and so would not have proposed to Margaret Schlegel. Charles sees Margaret's aim as being to get into Howards End at all costs. Thus he condemns her on moral grounds for having taken his mother's place.

Charles and Dolly are sitting in the garden of their home at Hilton; their small son and baby are with them, as well as the inevitable motorcar. Dolly is expecting a third child.

COMMENTARY: This is a humorous sketch of a couple. Forster has already shown Dolly's foolishness; her ways are those traditionally associated with some members of the 'weaker sex', very different from Forster's image of intelligence and femininity in the Schlegels. Egoism and self-interest are Charles's dominant features, and the close of the chapter pushes these to a humorous exaggeration worthy of the finest English parody. A Dickensian note is struck with the comic combination of the grandiose and the domestic.

## Chapter XXII

The morning after the rushed kiss, in Aunt Juley's garden, Helen has received a letter from Leonard to say that he is leaving the Porphyrion Company. Henry Wilcox says Porphyrion is 'not a bad business'. He has had a letter from Bryce who wants to sublet Howards End; he feels this is risky. Margaret ignores him, anxious about Leonard, who is going into a bank on a reduced salary. Henry says it is a secure job, so she agrees to discuss Howards End, but refuses to hurt Aunt Juley by cutting short her holiday to go to visit it. Henry insists masterfully; he will speak to Aunt Juley. It emerges that Porphyrion is now financially secure, and Helen is furious with Henry. He expounds his *laissez-faire* philosophy, then arranges with Aunt Juley for their visit to Howards End. Margaret placates Helen, saying that Henry is much nicer than his theories imply. She feels tenderness for him.

COMMENTARY: A new image emerges to evoke the 'Only connect . . . ' theme: the 'rainbow bridge', suggesting D.H. Lawrence (1885–1930) in his novel *The Rainbow* (1915). It coincides with a new aspect of this basic theme: Forster extends the inner and outer worlds of imagination and practical affairs to include the reconcilement of sex and spiritual life. The philosophy behind Henry's attitudes is elucidated in the conflict between his positivism and Helen's concern for the personal and individual.

## Chapter XXIII

Helen and Margaret talk about Helen's mysterious attitude to the engagement; Helen agrees to be as polite as she can, but still disagrees with Margaret. Now calmer, Margaret goes to London, to Henry's office in the West Africa Rubber Company. They go down to Hilton and have lunch at Dolly's. Henry is furious with Bryce for having left. At Howards End Henry goes to the farm to get the keys, but the door gives way when Margaret pushes it and she goes in. She hears a noise behind a door; throwing it open she sees a woman coming downstairs; for a moment she is taken by her for Ruth Wilcox. The old woman goes out into the rain.

COMMENTARY: Helen's belief in the subconscious contrasts with Margaret's increasing sense of a compromise between two concepts of life: simultaneously she is aware of the need to curb this sense of proportion, for it can spoil the spontaneity of existence, which Forster insists on. Africa is seen as a whale marked out for blubber, and Henry's radically changed attitude to his tenant develops those impressions of the Wilcox philosophy given in Chapter XXII. The difference between the two feminine characters is exposed by their diverse reactions to Henry's teasing.

NOTES AND GLOSSARY:

**Drayton:** Michael Drayton (1563–1631) wrote many pastoral poems. The poem referred to here is *Polyolbion*, on the beauty of England's countryside

## Chapter XXIV

Margaret and Henry go back to Dolly for tea, where Henry enjoys telling how frightened Margaret was by the 'apparition' of Miss Avery from the neighbouring farm. After travelling back to Wickham Place Margaret is relieved to find peace and calm; she is alone and can recapitulate, sensing the presence of nature and the past reaching her through Howards End and old Miss Avery.

COMMENTARY: Forster continues to emphasise the gap between Dolly's silly nature and Margaret's intelligence, both in the dialogue and remarks of his own as narrator. Margaret's discovery of nature springs from Howards End, which is thus enriched as a link with the past, and the wych-elm is an integral part of this. At the same time, Margaret gratefully sees Henry as one of those civilising influences that she refers to at the end of Chapter XIX.

## Chapter XXV

Her father's engagement is a shock to Evie; after family debates with Dolly and Charles she advances her wedding from September to August. Margaret finds herself with seven others on a train journey; they are to meet Charles at Shrewsbury and continue by car to Henry's house in Oniton, Shropshire, for Evie's wedding. At Shrewsbury, Margaret goes sight-seeing in one of the cars; then they all leave, escorted by a very business-like Charles. The car Margaret is in hits something and stops; a girl comes screaming out of a cottage, and the women are put into another car which goes ahead, leaving the men to settle matters. Margaret, resenting the masculine organisation, jumps out of the car and falls on her knees. She wishes to go and help; it turns out to be a cat that has been killed. She reluctantly gets back into the second car; all has been arranged. On arrival she tells all this to Henry, using her feminine charm; Charles and Henry draw their own conclusions. Later, Charles, out on the hill beside the house, worrying about family finances, sees Margaret out too, and imagines for a moment that she has come to entice him. She goes in, calling out in the darkness her love of the place.

COMMENTARY: Forster compresses a social group into a train journey; the overwhelming pressure of masculine society pushes Margaret into individual reaction, asserting her independence by visiting Shrewsbury, and refusing to accept male supremacy on the road to Oniton. Yet her subsequent account to Henry is an excellent example of feminine wile and condescension, showing a spirit of compromise totally lacking in Helen.

NOTES AND GLOSSARY:

**Tariff Reform:** a controversy of the day opposing Free Traders and Tariff Reformers who wanted a protective system for imperial goods

## Chapter XXVI

Margaret loves Oniton, strolls around it. After the wedding reception she joins Henry in the meadow to relax. From afar she notices new arrivals, and is surprised to discover Helen and the Basts. The Basts are penniless, Leonard having lost his job. Margaret, displeased, agrees to co-operate by asking Henry if he can find him work. They are to sleep as her guests at the hotel. She returns to Henry, who is still in the meadow; he agrees to help. They go back to the garden and Henry discovers Jacky, his mistress of ten years before. Margaret, shaken, thinks of Ruth Wilcox, and sees off a wedding guest.

COMMENTARY: As the relationship between Margaret and Henry deepens Margaret's range of behaviour becomes wider. Tiny details show up the incongruities of the feminine and masculine worlds. Compromise follows upon compromise; details such as the two men smiling at her remarks in the wine-cellar, her courtesy as hostess with the guests, and her deliberate use of the 'harem' methods, all point to this contrast. Woman is complementary to man, not a rebel, she realises; yet Margaret is at home with paradoxical truths, knowing also that a man with a 'shadowy' wife is at a disadvantage. One of the most extravagant coincidences, Henry and Jacky's liaison, here introduces a further complication, linking the three groups of people, the three classes, closer together in the plot.

NOTES AND GLOSSARY:

**Durbar:** an official reception in India, given by an Indian prince or the British governor-general

## Chapter XXVII

Helen wonders why she has spent so much money on making people angry. In the coffee-room of the hotel she and Leonard, his wife gone to bed, chat together. Helen asks him about himself and Jacky, guessing at his unhappiness. Leonard feels much fonder of Helen than of Margaret. He is disillusioned about his cultural activities, having given them up because of lack of time and money. Helen explains her concept of self-awareness, and in reply to Leonard's realistic assertions on the necessity of money she cites death as the supreme reality.

COMMENTARY: The focus shifts; after many episodes devoted to Margaret, Helen is here the centre of attention. Her remarks on self-awareness and death are prophetic, and will find later echoes in the narrative.

NOTES AND GLOSSARY:

**Pierpont Morgan:** John Pierpont Morgan (1837–1913), the American art collector and civic benefactor

## Chapter XXVIII

Margaret is stunned at first, so she does nothing. Then she tries to write letters. The first one, to Henry, declares her love and understanding; she tears it up, feeling miserable. Her note to Leonard says that her husband has no vacancy for him, and a note to Helen tells her to come round and sleep at the house, that the Basts are not worth the trouble. Her main anxiety is that Helen should not learn about Henry's liaison. She leaves these notes in the hotel; on her return she meets Henry in the hall, and they speak as if nothing had happened. She says that she would like Helen to come and sleep in the house, and goes up to bed. She feels love and pity for Henry, hoping to help him.

COMMENTARY: Margaret's confused thoughts ultimately lead to the same feelings as she has always had for Henry: affection mixed with pity; and a steady conviction that her love will change him. In her response to the situation she is most objective; it is for his own sake that Henry should give her explanations. This is a further and striking example of her reasonable, intelligent approach to affairs of the heart.

NOTES AND GLOSSARY:

**saturnalia:** in Roman religion, the festival of Saturn, celebrated in mid-December, a week of feasting and licence for all classes, even slaves

## Chapter XXIX

At breakfast Margaret expresses her forgiveness, which shocks Henry. He prefers a dramatic scene, in order to deserve her and rebuild an image of masculine dignity and strength. Her frank acceptance is too much; she must have been reading literature intended for men only! He recounts everything; it happened ten years ago in a garrison town in Cyprus. Henry, fearing blackmail, asks Margaret to swear secrecy. The Basts and Helen have left already, and their silence worries Margaret. Henry and she leave Oniton, never to return there.

COMMENTARY: Through his use of coincidence Forster has exposed Margaret and Henry to a tricky confrontation between past and present.

Tiny details express the psychology of each, while also repeating an act in the man-woman drama. Henry plays within the limited range of emotion we associate with him, whereas Margaret is stretched to new dimensions, demonstrating the scope of her mature approach. An unusual observation for a male author is Forster's suggestion of the same fleeting physical attraction felt by women for men as Margaret, listening to Henry's 'confession', looks appreciatively at the handsome butler. Forster speaks for women here, reiterating an age-old inequality; Henry would have been outraged. Notice the image of grass running through Margaret's fingers, part of the recurrent motif of hay and an anticipation, too, of the sensation she has at the end of Chapter XLIII, as she drives her fingers through grass.

NOTES AND GLOSSARY:
**See the Conquering Hero:** a quotation from *Joshua*, Part iii, by
                Dr Thomas Morell (1703–84)

## Chapter XXX

Tibby is in his last year at Oxford. Having sent a telegram Helen goes to see him. She is upset, tells him about Jacky and Henry, and the visit to Oniton. Tibby is rather bored; personal problems do not interest him. She asks him to decide if Margaret should be told of Henry's past liaison. She also asks him to pay compensation to Leonard for having lost his job, as she is going to Germany. She will leave five thousand pounds available for this. Margaret, the next day, learns from Tibby that Helen is aware of Henry's liaison. Tibby sends Leonard a first cheque of one hundred pounds, and a note about the rest. Leonard replies, refusing both the cheque and the legacy. Tibby goes to Leonard's address to find that Leonard and Jacky have been evicted for not paying the rent. Helen later reinvests her money.

COMMENTARY: Two things are put to proof: Tibby's indifferent, self-contained nature and Helen's theories of the Chelsea debates. Helen's impulsive, sincere response to life comes out in her generous gesture. Leonard's refusal is manly.

## Chapter XXXI

Wickham Place is gradually emptied of its furniture and finally knocked down in the autumn. The furniture mostly goes to Howards End, the tenant having died abroad. Henry will later re-let it.

Margaret and Henry are married and spend their honeymoon near Innsbruck. Margaret hoped that Helen would come to see them, but receives a post-card from Lake Garda, saying her plans are vague.

Margaret replies, saying that sexual matters need understanding, as she supposes Helen resents Henry's behaviour. A strange reply comes back; Helen is going to Naples for the winter. Henry is relieved, not yet ready to meet Helen. He tells Margaret of having sold Oniton to a preparatory school, as it was damp. They live in the Ducie Street house for the winter, hoping to find a new house in the spring. They settle into a routine; Margaret is no longer interested in cultural activities.

COMMENTARY: The flux, represented here by the demolition of Wickham Place and the temporary residence in Ducie Street, contrasts with the steady nature of Margaret's calm relationship with Henry, and her pursuit of inward life as she turns away from the stimulus of intellectual outings.

## Chapter XXXII

In the spring Margaret is looking over plans for a house that they have decided to build in Sussex. Dolly arrives. Margaret is anxious about Helen, away eight months; her address is poste restante in Bavaria. Dolly is less vivacious and is worried about money, as Henry leaves them to fend for themselves. She tells Margaret about an incident over a wedding present from Miss Avery to Evie: Evie had refused it and insulted Miss Avery. The Wilcoxes had interpreted Miss Avery's gift as an attempt to get invited to the wedding; when Margaret suggests it may have been in remembrance of Ruth Wilcox, Dolly agrees weakly. Dolly also tells her that Miss Avery has unpacked some of the Schlegels' things, particularly books. Considering the misunderstanding with Miss Avery, Margaret decides it preferable that she herself should go down to Howards End to see her.

COMMENTARY: Dolly's conversation appears as an echo of the men around her, in contrast to Margaret's independent opinions. A sociological view is given in this chapter of the Wilcox notions regarding class and finance.

## Chapter XXXIII

Margaret enjoys rediscovering Hilton on a spring day. At the farm she is received very ceremoniously by Miss Avery's niece. At Howards End, Miss Avery will not open the door until her niece has left. Margaret is amazed to see all the rooms furnished with the furniture and belongings from Wickham Place. Angry at first, she then feels the poetical logic of it. Miss Avery, hoping to revive the old house, has even prepared a nursery. She loved Ruth Wilcox, but dislikes the men,

and tells Margaret of their tendency to get hay fever. Margaret consults
Henry, who advises storage in London. Before she can do this, unexpected trouble comes.

COMMENTARY: Forster's association of ideas and landscape is a good
introduction to Miss Avery, a natural aristocrat of old stock. She
comes into her own as a force connecting with England's past, and her
action brings Howards End and all it stands for into the foreground.
The reader hesitates with Margaret under the impact of the momentary
sense of permanence.

NOTES AND GLOSSARY:

**Chapel of Ease:**   chapel built for the convenience of worshippers
who live at some distance from the parish church.
This passage recalls Martin Luther (1483–1546) in
his *Table Talk of God's Works*: 'For, where God
built a church, there the Devil would also build a
chapel.'

## Chapter XXXIV

Aunt Juley has pneumonia; Margaret and Tibby go to Swanage, sending
a telegram to Helen. Margaret fears her aunt is dying, and the novelist
exploits this fear, then suddenly announces her recovery. Margaret's
anxiety about Helen increases, as Helen has telegraphed in reply that
she can only come for a short time. Margaret begins to suspect mental
trouble, arising from the incident with Paul. A letter comes the day of
Aunt Juley's recovery: Helen will be in London the following day, and
will leave her address at the bank. Margaret is tempted to oblige her to
come down by telling her Aunt Juley is still in danger, but decides
against this, and replies with the truth. Helen's telegram answer asks
where their furniture is stored, but Margaret refuses to tell her, asking
her to meet her at the bank at four o'clock. She and Tibby do not find
her there, and are refused her address when they ask for it. They drop
into St Paul's Cathedral on the way to Henry's office. Reluctantly, on
Henry's advice, Margaret writes a letter to Helen, saying she can see
the furniture the following Monday at Howards End; the plan is that
they will 'ambush' her there.

COMMENTARY: Forster enjoys creating suspense and then declaring Aunt Juley's recovery. Margaret's reflection on the effect of
Paul's kiss on Helen is in keeping with contemporary psychology in
the significance it gives to a past incident, and it leads to an interesting
metaphorical image of the narrator's, considering the 'seed' of experience.

## Chapter XXXV

A lovely spring day, the following Monday. At Hilton Margaret and Henry hear that Helen has arrived. They lunch at Dolly's, and Margaret is overcome by it all. While she is in the lavatory Henry slips out to go to Howards End alone, but Dolly's child is playing in the middle of the path, so Crane, the chauffeur, is obliged to slow down. Margaret jumps into the car, resenting the dishonesty of her scheme to catch Helen, and annoyed with Henry. These feelings increase when they pick up the doctor, Mansbridge, who asks questions which prompt Henry to discuss Helen's character. She sees Helen in the porch, sitting with her back to them. She goes quickly to her, shutting the garden gate in Henry's face. Helen is pregnant. Margaret unlocks Howards End and pushes Helen inside.

COMMENTARY: The traditional image of a pastoral English springtime opens the chapter, linking it with previous visits to Howards End, but this time cruel irony is in the promise of spring. Forster's conscious art as narrator creating surprise for the reader is in his portrait of Helen, framed in the doorway, her back to oncomers. Henry's enjoyment of his well-organised scheme is an excellent expression of how his business attitudes intervene at all levels of his existence, even in emotional situations.

## Chapter XXXVI

Margaret now stands with her back to the door, facing the men and holding the bunch of keys. The driver of the fly in which Helen arrived tells the doctor of Helen's condition, and the doctor whispers to Henry, who looks horrified. Margaret refuses to let them see Helen. They give up; she tells Henry that she will see him later at Dolly's. The car moves off and she goes in, begging Helen to forgive her scheming.

COMMENTARY: Margaret's stance between Helen and the men is most symbolic. She epitomises the underlying theme of women's autonomy as individuals in society, an echo of Forster's earlier statements on the importance of this over and above even the collective movement for women's rights, which he viewed less favourably. Margaret does not care about 'rights', but absolutely refuses the men access to Helen. Forster shows his well-known dislike of doctors here. The metaphorical interpretation of the whole scheme compares it to a hunt; as in Chapter XXXV, where the car was like a 'beast of prey', so here the men are called a 'pack'.

## Chapter XXXVII

Margaret and Helen find it difficult to speak to each other at first; Helen is living with an Italian girl in Munich; her baby is to be born in June. They chat casually about childhood incidents, recalled by the furniture. They feel very close; the 'inner life had paid'. A boy, Tom, calls with milk sent by Miss Avery. They open up the house, and Helen decides that they should stay the night. Margaret hesitates, wondering about Henry's, and particularly, Charles's reactions. She goes to consult Henry, noticing Tom playing in the straw.

COMMENTARY: The emotional core of the novel is here, where the relationship between the two sisters shifts back to its centre and gradually asserts its unique quality. Verging on sentimentality, it is saved by the solid metaphorical support in the union between past and present in Wickham Place and Howards End. The feeling of permanence is pervasive and heightened by the vision of Tom in the straw, a significant detail rooted in Forster's own life.

## Chapter XXXVIII

Margaret arrives at Dolly's; Henry is waiting on the lawn. He wants to know if Helen has a wedding-ring, who her seducer is. He has contacted Charles and Tibby. Margaret is feeling weak, but stands firm. She asks if Helen may stay the night at Howards End; Henry refuses on grounds of dampness, his position in society, and finally on principles of respect for his deceased wife. Margaret loses patience; she reminds him of his hypocrisy, of her earlier forgiveness. He had a mistress during Ruth's lifetime, and yet cites her memory when refusing his house for one night to Helen. Accusing Margaret of blackmailing him over the Bast affair, he goes in. Margaret leaves.

COMMENTARY: Margaret's easy, accommodating ways with Henry are now useless. The principle on which he asserts his authority is an ancient one, and maintains a basic inequality between man and woman. Although the logic of his citing the memory of his wife is as absurd as Margaret points out, such reactions are so common that he merely appears as a caricature of family hypocrisy.

## Chapter XXXIX

Charles and Tibby meet briefly at Ducie Street. Tibby is better off than Charles, being an intellectual living, in a leisurely way, on an income. Charles raises his voice, asking all kinds of questions, and Tibby blushes when he asks him who the seducer may be. Tibby is thinking of

Helen's visit to Oxford, and mentions Leonard. Feeling ashamed, he advances no more information and Charles leaves.

COMMENTARY: As in the preceding scene between Margaret and Henry, the Wilcox aggressiveness gives them a tactical advantage, and contrasts with Schlegel intelligence. Tibby's lack of resistance, unlike Margaret's resilience, proves his fundamental indifference.

## Chapter XL

We are told that Leonard will figure in a newspaper report. Meanwhile, under the wych-elm, Helen tells Margaret of how she and Leonard made love at the Oniton hotel. She describes it as assuaging the disturbance caused in her by Paul. Margaret does not tell her of the upset with Henry; this is Helen's night. Margaret notices the pigs' teeth gleaming; she and Helen talk of Ruth Wilcox's pervasive presence. Miss Avery appears, then disappears, through a gap in the hedge which Henry had filled in, separating Howards End and the farm. Helen suggests that Margaret should go with her to Germany and Margaret considers the possibility. They go to bed; Margaret stays awake, wondering if Leonard also springs from Ruth Wilcox's mind.

COMMENTARY: The narrator creates suspense concerning Leonard. 'Only connect' is given its most profound and poetical interpretation here as the two girls talk under the wych-elm, the pigs' teeth, absurd yet vital relics, gleaming. The moonlight also illuminates the sword which belonged to the Schlegels' father, hung on the wall by Miss Avery, and still to play a role. Leonard's night with Helen, seen as an accomplishment of her experience with Paul, materialises Forster's, and Margaret's, theories of psychology in Chapter XXXIV.

## Chapter XLI

Leonard, since Oniton, has been tortured by remorse. Financially he and Jacky have survived by shaming his family into supporting them. Even when his brother-in-law found him work, he refused it, having become one of the unemployable. He sees Margaret and Tibby in St Paul's but does not approach them. Realising that they were worried about Helen he tracks them down to Ducie Street, calling the day Margaret has gone to Howards End. The next morning he arrives at Howards End and is attacked by Charles with the flat of the Schlegel sword. They lay him outside, dead. Miss Avery comes out, carrying the sword.

COMMENTARY: The sharp-cutting edge of a blade, suggested by the moonlit sword and traditionally malevolent, is continued in the metaphorical imagery of Leonard's remorse. The malevolence of the sword reaches its culmination at the close of the chapter. Death is dramatic but expressed in simple language as in the case of Ruth Wilcox, confronting the reader with the sudden, unpredictable element in life.

NOTES AND GLOSSARY:

**Erinyes:** in classical mythology they were female divinities, avengers of iniquity. They were not vindictive; their punishments were impartial

**And if I drink ...:** a quotation from *Modern Love* (1862), ch. xii, a novelette in pseudo sonnet-sequence form by George Meredith (1828–1909), in which he deals with incompatibility of temper

## Chapter XLII

After seeing Tibby in Ducie Street Charles had gone home to Hilton. There is no sign of Margaret all evening; Henry, after midnight, goes to Charles's room, telling him the girls are sleeping at Howards End. Charles will go up the following morning, but must use no violence. Charles, on his return after Leonard's death, explains how the man was in the last stages of heart disease, and how he had attacked him only with the flat of the blade. After such a scandal Charles thinks he will be obliged to leave Hilton. He wants to drive his father to the police station, but Henry goes on foot. When he returns he is very tired. There is to be an inquest the next day; Charles will be the most important witness.

COMMENTARY: The Wilcox self-confidence in their own philosophy supports both the men: Henry, less concerned by the quarrel with Margaret than by the girls' sleeping at Howards End, can share this problem with his son: Charles, like his father, builds up a protective optimism against the future. The motor-car, expressive of modernity, shows up Charles's loss of contact with reality here.

## Chapter XLIII

Margaret feels at sea in the series of strange events, yet she is aware of the spiritual significance behind them. Helen tries to keep calm for the baby's sake. Margaret has to face questionings from officials, among whom is Dr Mansbridge who agrees that Leonard's death was due to heart disease. Body and sword are taken to Hilton. Margaret decides she will go to Germany. Crane, the chauffeur, comes to take her to meet Henry outside Charles's home, in the road. They sit on a bank. He is weary; Charles is about to be prosecuted for manslaughter. She feels neither warmth nor aggression, just a sudden sensation of life in the ground under her. Charles is sentenced to three years' imprisonment. Henry breaks down; she takes him to Howards End.

COMMENTARY: Margaret's capacity to see beyond superficial reality helps her now as a source of strength; she does not lose sight of the inner world. Abstract concepts sustain her, and orientate her response to situations. This inner reality is suddenly incarnated by the live contact she makes with nature.

## Chapter XLIV

Tom plays with Helen's baby, while Tom's father is cutting the meadow. It is fourteen months since the events of the preceding chapter. Margaret has decided to stay on at Howards End. The Wilcoxes are all together in the house, except Charles who is in prison. Helen admits affection for Henry, but says that she herself will never marry. Margaret says that she never wants a child; people are different. Helen recognises how, thanks to Margaret, they are all happy and united. They sense how this permanence will change, how urban life is creeping into the countryside. Paul comes out, aggressive, asking for Margaret to go in. Henry is consulting the family in order to put his will in a final form. Margaret will have the house but wants no money. Henry will render his children independent by giving them the money; this is Margaret's wish. Margaret sees them out, then goes back to Henry who explains Dolly's parting remark about Margaret's having been left Howards End. She is shocked to hear this, but is calm. Helen comes in with her baby. She tells them that the meadow is mown and the crop will be plentiful.

COMMENTARY: Helen recognises Margaret for what she is: the central force who has united the family and made life pleasant for those who had seemed broken by events, herself and Henry. The final irony of the whole novel emerges: Ruth Wilcox's scribbled message has been fulfilled; and while Margaret will ensure the survival of Howards End, Leonard's child will give it a future.

# Part 3

# Commentary

## Early sources of *Howards End*

No matter what trends in literary criticism may say, today or tomorrow, about the relevance of biography, the reader should not neglect the origin of *Howards End*. The text, in this case, is witness to the vital link between the mature novelist and formative episodes of his childhood, and as such, vindicates Forster's underlying maxim: 'Only connect...' The house Howards End is directly inspired by Rooksnest, where Forster lived from 1883 to 1893. The choice of name too, is associated with this childhood home, for it once belonged to a family called Howard. As a schoolboy at Tonbridge, Forster made a 'sentimental inventory of its rooms',* and some of the features in this are exploited by the novelist. Rooksnest was a 'charming house, with its rosy brickwork, its ancient vine' (p.16).

Helen's first letter immediately establishes the pattern of associations between the real and fictional houses, mentioning as it does, the 'red brick' and the 'beautiful vine leaves'. The two houses share many other characteristics. Helen's letter also describes the three bedrooms in a row upstairs, and above them the three attics, and Rooksnest was similarly designed. In Forster's inventory we read that there was one beam across the ceiling in most of the rooms, and this fact is mentioned in Chapter XXIII of *Howards End*. Another precise detail, and one which Forster uses to dramatic ends, is the door to the stairs. It must have impressed the young boy with a kind of awe, and in his notes he describes it: '... the door to the staircase which was thus quite shut in and could not be found by new people, who wondered how ever we got up' (p.16). This mystery of a hidden staircase felt by the child later finds artistic expression in Chapter XXIII when Margaret flings open the same door to discover Miss Avery, who, for a brief moment, takes her to be Ruth Wilcox. Thus the direct correspondence existing between a particular physical detail and a childhood feeling is exploited by the novelist to the full, as he extends and develops the concrete reality of the door to sustain the abstract mystery of Ruth Wilcox's pervading presence.

* P.N. Furbank, *E.M. Forster: a Life*, 2 vols, Secker & Warburg, London, 1978, vol. 1, p.16. Further page references to this volume are given after quotations in the text. Forster's notes on Rooksnest also appear as an appendix to the Penguin edition of *Howards End*.

A striking incongruity occurs, too, which denotes how the author's memory of something as it was can come into conflict with a later modified version of it within the structure of the novel. In his notes, Forster remembers an old pond, which his mother had got drained, and which was known as the 'dell 'ole' (p.17). In Chapter XXIII Margaret notices how: 'Down by the dell-hole more vivid colours were awakening.' The definite article here recaptures the child's memory of a single and unique reality, and yet this disappears at the end of the novel, when the word has lost its original, singular aspect: 'Close by them a man was preparing to scythe out one of the dell-holes.'

'Dell 'ole' is the local pronunciation as it is in Forster's notes, and there is another word which appears in the novel in its local rendering, and as with the dell-hole, forms part of the intricate network of childhood memories. The 'meadow' is in Helen's letter, as are other surrounding features of the original house – elm trees, dog-roses, a neighbouring farm. The meadow recurs in the narrative many times, and ultimately emerges as having a 'sacred centre' in the final chapter. It is in Chapter XXXIII that it takes on local colour in Miss Avery's words: 'Yes, the maidy's well enough.' In his notes Forster quotes the farmer beside Rooksnest, to whom his mother rented the meadow, as having said on the last of his visits to pay the rent: 'Well, well, it's been a dear maidy' (p.18).

Such fragments as these are essential indications of Forster's deliberate transcription of the past in *Howards End*; sometimes they are enhanced by spiritual associations, as in the case of the meadow at the close of the novel, or that of the wych-elm, which takes on an aura of ancient folklore. The teeth were in the original one, and the wych-elm was obviously singled out by the young Forster because of this strange phenomenon, and the tree's immensity:

> It was of great height and had a very thick stem, but the curious part in it was this. About four feet from the ground were three or four fangs stuck deep into the rugged bark. As far as I can make out these were votive offerings of people who had their toothache cured by chewing pieces of bark, but whether they were their own teeth I don't know and certainly it does not seem likely that they should sacrifice one sound tooth as the price of having one aching one cured. (p.18)

That Rooksnest remained as a vital part of Forster's imagination when later living in suburban houses is evident in the dimension he gives it in *Howards End*. The idyllic times he associates it with are present in the lyrical evocations of nature, and especially spring, which often accompany its recurrent appearances throughout the text, and these times are perhaps epitomised in the vision of summer hay-making at the end. An earlier suggestion of this vision is the image of children playing in the straw in Chapter XXXIII. Again, Forster's childhood emerges, for one of his most precious memories was of those preschool days when he simply enjoyed playing in the hay with the neighbour's son Frankie. This remained with him all his life as a kind of paradisaic epoch; he never forgot it, often returning there, and he writes of these visits to the place:

> I have kept in touch with it, going back to it as to an abiding city and still visiting the house which was once my home, for it is occupied by friends. A farm is through the hedge, and when the farmer there was eight years old and I was nine, we used to jump up and down on his grandfather's straw ricks and spoil them.*

These visits to his old home are emblematic of the novelist's attempts to recreate the past through the language and narrative structure of his work.

In this correspondence between Howards End and its prototype one common trait comes to light: each detail of the original, given a very concrete presence in Forster's prolific notes, takes on a much deeper significance when integrated within the imaginative texture of his imagery, and assumes symbolical dimensions. The very real mystery of the young Forster's experience becomes even more mysterious when it is enriched by its inclusion within the novel. This enrichment of remembered features of Rooksnest is achieved by the novelist's dramatic presentation of the door leading to the stairs, or by his emphasis on particular features such as the wych-elm or the house itself. Through this particular exercise of the writer's art Forster's introductory words 'Only connect . . .' find their most vital realisation; imagination is the communicatory agent, transforming the concise details of those notes into an integral work of art. The close of *Howards End* is a poetical consummation of the past: within the narrative, as within a piece of music, diverse elements have come together in unison. There is no one better than Forster himself to illuminate this process by drawing a parallel with music:

> Expansion. That is the idea the novelist must cling to. Not completion. Not rounding off but opening out. When the symphony is over we feel that the notes and tunes composing it have been liberated, they have found in the rhythm of the whole their individual freedom.†

The last words in the case of this work are Helen's, thus closing a circle

---

* E.M. Forster, *Two Cheers for Democracy*, Edward Arnold, London, 1951, p.69.
† E.M. Forster, *Aspects of the Novel*, Edward Arnold, London, 1927, p.216.

that opened with Helen's epistolary evocation of the house; these words, as Forster's parallel here implies, open onto that future which is contained within the past. As in music, a resonance continues the theme beyond the conclusion of the work itself, and thus the infinite, circular image of the field's 'sacred centre'.

# Characterisation

## Ruth Wilcox

Ruth Wilcox does not play an obviously active role in the narrative, and unlike other major characters she makes very little impression through dialogue; what is more, she dies early in the novel. None the less, she is a very strong and pervasive presence, even after her death. This is conveyed rather by a pattern of associations than by any specific characteristics.

She first appears in Helen's letter, framed by nature as in an impressionist painting; the rhythm of her patient way of living is portrayed by Helen's image of her 'watching the large red poppies come out'. It is Ruth who introduces the motif of hay, an essential link throughout the novel and rendering her an implicit part of the spiritual affirmation at the close of the novel. Her hands are full of fresh-cut hay in Helen's letter, and she comes into the narrative in Chapter III carrying a 'wisp of hay', and the chapter concludes with her smelling a rose. These two images of flower and hay come together later, and she actually becomes them, 'she was a wisp of hay, a flower'; as such she is in juxtaposition to the Wilcox males, the 'social counterpart of a motor-car' as Forster says of her in the same passage (Chapter IX).

Ruth's incarnation as flowers and hay has metaphorical implications, connecting her with the repetitive pattern of life, death and the seasons that transpires from Helen's final speech at the end of the novel. Nowhere is Forster so explicit about her significance as in Chapter III, where she represents perennial values, spiritual fulfilment as opposed to the 'panic and emptiness' of modern life.

Ruth is thus indissolubly linked with Howards End and the garden, in particular the wych-elm, belonging 'not to the young people and their motor, but to the house, and to the tree that overshadowed it', and she possesses 'that wisdom to which we give the clumsy name of aristocracy'. Later, Margaret asserts this link between Ruth, the house and the tree, and she simultaneously recognises Ruth as the holder of a superior knowledge: 'I cannot believe that knowledge such as hers will perish with knowledge such as mine' (Chapter XL). Already, during Ruth's lifetime, Margaret has sensed this, when Ruth, as a quiet and non-intellectual guest at her luncheon-party, is paradoxically the one who leaves the most haunting impression after she has gone. Ruth's characteristic resignation and patience come to light as she welcomes Evie and Henry, who have spoilt her cherished project of bringing Margaret to Howards End. Although 'imagination' could not 'triumph' this time, and she soon dies, there is an ultimate triumph for Ruth when fate ironically fulfils her written wish by giving Howards End to Margaret. Thus, as an almost prophetic presence, it is hardly surprising that Ruth's character is possibly the mainspring of the narrative.

Like the house itself, Ruth Wilcox comes from the author's personal experience; on a nostalgic visit to Rooksnest in 1906, Forster called on neighbours, the Postons, to discover that Mr Poston had remarried. It was the fundamental incompatibility in the couple that struck him, and became the seed of the Wilcox family, as Forster's notes in Furbank's biography imply:

> Mr. P. looked very well indeed, but his voice is awful—a loud whisper.... Like all such, he talks incessantly. The wife is so charming—pretty, pleasant, clever, and the Jowitts say so good and kind as well. She seems terribly incongruous there. (p.142)

## Margaret Schlegel

Ruth Wilcox is the dominant spirit of ancient wisdom, and Margaret's trajectory through the narrative will ultimately lead her to become Ruth Wilcox's spiritual heiress; she not only inherits Howards End as Ruth wanted her to, but she also assumes a similar role as the patient, loving centre in the group of people living there. To come to this she gradually evolves, and as the plot unfolds, her character reveals its multiple depths.

Growing up with Helen in a cosmopolitan and erudite atmosphere, Margaret's intelligence is cultivated. Her most striking quality, perhaps, and source of her inner resilience, is a kind of persistent lucidity; this emerges as she comes to adulthood, along with her awareness of spiritual, 'personal' forces, and her conclusion is that any individual 'lies nearer to the unseen than any organization' (Chapter IV). This attitude is at the root of her liberalism, her later rejection of the collective which she expresses in the Chelsea discussion group. Margaret's imagination is more restrained than her sister's; unlike Helen, for whom Beethoven's symphony is full of 'heroes and shipwrecks' Margaret 'can only see the music'. This implies her objective tendency to see things for what they are. None the less, she cannot live without attending concerts and discussion societies. It is only later, after her involvement with Henry, that Margaret begins to turn inwards, abandoning her multiple intellectual activities for a more tangible emotional contact, outgrowing 'stimulants' and moving from 'words to things' (Chapter XXXI).

Margaret's need to reconcile the outer and inner forces becomes more urgent, particularly under pressure of Henry's imperviousness, which acts as a challenge. Her decisive nature helps her to resolve predicaments life puts before her; at so many stages in the novel she must make up her mind, reacting to a situation. Forster's appraisal of her mental processes is very precise: 'Her mind darted from impulse to impulse, and finally marshalled them all in review' (Chapter VIII). Sometimes she is caught in a stream of events, and reacts with spontaneous determination. Two impulsive gestures in particular show up this complementary side of her nature, and they are strangely similar: she jumps out of the moving car on the way to Evie's wedding, and later jumps on to a moving car in Dolly's garden in Chapter XXXV. In both of these cases she is defending her role as an individual and as a woman against the overbearing dominance of the male in society. Her final diatribe against Henry in Chapter XXXVIII is delivered after many months of forbearance, and is a plea for reciprocity between man and woman.

Margaret's striving after unity between the material and the spiritual is not only an intellectual predicament reflecting Forster's awareness of a fundamental dichotomy, but she must also try to unite the 'beast and the monk' through her union with Henry (Chapter XXII). As she turns inwards, away from intellectual activities, she finds herself in a kind of constant alternation: at first she quite enjoys shifting between her independent self and condescending to play the feminine game. This gives the novelist an opportunity for a humorous study of duplicity within woman as partner to man. At first she is excited by his masculinity, but soon this novelty gives way to loving patience and hope. Because of Henry's dense obtuseness she never really 'connects' with him, and the whole question of physical and spiritual union is as if left in abeyance. However, like Ruth Wilcox before her, she 'connects' with nature; the decisive moment is an instinctive response within herself when a 'new life began to move' (Chapter XLIII).

## Helen Schlegel

Helen's most distinctive characteristic, and conveyed by dialogue, is perhaps her whimsical humour, and certainly one of the fundamental contrasts between herself and Margaret lies in their different uses of language. Helen, as the more creative, imaginative sister, uses language as a resource of fantasy and wit; she employs lively imagery, and evidently enjoys words for their own sake.

As the younger, more attractive of the two sisters, Helen's reaction to the Wilcox masculinity at first is in keeping with her femininity. She is not only won over by the masculine atmosphere, abandoning her intellectual ideals, but she is also enticed by the material comfort and the motor-car especially, a recurrent motif of modernity and masculinity. Disillusioned to find Paul so weak, her admiration turns to revulsion, and when the opportunity comes to confirm her aversion for Henry she does so with a vengeance. In so far as Margaret is a voluntary personality, Helen seems by contrast much more passive. Her sexual awakening with Paul becomes a memory that lives on, and she herself admits her night with Leonard was a kind of reaction to the earlier experience (Chapter XL). Her maternity is the culmination of her passiveness, revealing her as the epitome of feminine receptivity. Her very attractiveness and youth make her a ready prey of fate, as Forster warns us at the end of Chapter IV, whereas Margaret as an older, more mature and less attractive woman has a better hold on life.

Once disillusioned with the Wilcoxes, Helen turns away from the outer life of 'telegrams and anger'. This reaction will push her over to the other extreme, and Margaret's balanced view of things is contrasted with Helen's extremism in Chapter XXIII. Forster himself probably feared such excessive emotionalism, and preferred to recognise a certain indebtedness to those who had a hold on 'the ropes'. Helen, at the other end of the scale, defends the unseen, inner passions, knowing she can never compromise like her sister. As a passive, receptive person she retains experience and realises, more than any other character, the passage of time as it is felt subjectively. One tiny detail emblematic of this is the connection she makes between the greengage tree and the past through Evie's dumb-bells (Chapter XXXVII), but there is a much deeper, Freudian dimension to her attachment to past experience underlying her relationship with Leonard. In discussing Helen's memory of Paul, Forster elaborates on a metaphorical image of the mind as a 'seed-bed' for which subconscious forces leave one powerless to choose the 'seed', which then propagates, linking past to present, sometimes with disastrous consequences (Chapter XXXIV).

The isolation and courage which define Helen's life after her experience with Leonard would seem complementary to that audacious, intuitive strength which Margaret senses and almost fears in her, feeling she was a 'little unbalanced' (Chapter XXIII). However, the 'inner life had paid', and the sisters are united at the close. Helen's youth and resourceful spirit give the book its last words, and in them there is a joyful acceptance of the seasons, significant in one who has known with the passing of time painful experience. Opening and closing the narrative, and introducing each time the image of hay, Helen plays the role of a spiritual witness, a Martha opposite her counterpart.

## Henry Wilcox

Henry Wilcox represents masculinity, and is typical of a particular social class, the emergent Tory business class of the end of the nineteenth century. His masculinity is on two levels: first, it is an aura surrounding him, created by a specific background, by specific symbols, and constitutes a large part of the 'outer' world in the novel; on a second level, it is in Henry's own psychological make-up, especially when brought into play against Margaret's personality.

Henry's masculinity is a pervasive quality, dependent to a large extent on his property, of which the car is the most succinct image, and which connects Henry as a rich businessman with the general incursion of modernity. When he makes his first direct appearance, very briefly at the railway station, he and his car seem to form an entity against a backward world. His physique is most revealing of his personality: the image of his forehead as a 'bastion' expresses masculine strength and a tendency to be on the defensive, and as the author suggests this is not necessarily a sign of inner strength, merely saying that there was no 'external hint of weakness' (Chapter XI).

In Chapter XXIX, a crucial moment for Henry, the notion of 'fortress' evokes a masculine aura sheltering Henry from direct contact with life. Margaret is his accomplice, aware of the male psychology involved, and so plays the 'girl', waiting until Henry recovers himself sufficiently to 'rebuild his fortress and hide his soul'. Soon, Henry is back to being the hub of that middle-class universe, where he takes no time to feel emotion; he is objective, acting on the world of things around him in Oniton, just as his business imperialist world acts on the map of Africa in his office. He has a totally different concept of time from Helen's, his most feminine counterpart in the novel, and in opposition to him at moments. Whilst she is absorbed by emotions within the passage of time, so he exploits it, living out the famous business maxim of time being money; 'a little Ten Minutes moving self-contained through its appointed years' is how Forster describes his mind (Chapter XXIX).

The philosophy behind such activity is aggressive self-survival and the positivist doctrine of *laissez-faire* in economic matters, as expounded by a complacent Henry to a shocked Helen in Chapter XXII. When Helen comes to grips with him in an argument, Henry's confidence is seen to lie in the impersonal forces, a direct juxtaposition to Helen's adherence to the personal forces in life. Ironically, despite this show of strength, Henry will be considerably weakened by the end of the book, and it is his obtuseness, his failure to 'connect' with the personal forces, which are at the root of his moral collapse.

At moments we get a glimpse of decency in Henry, as in his attitude to Margaret during the discussion of the will in Chapter XI, when he

shows a fair-mindedness lacking totally in Charles, who seems a caricature of his father's most negative features.

## Leonard Bast

Leonard Bast is cleverly introduced into the narrative in the same chapter as the concert; drawn towards art, but living in difficult circumstances, he alternates between the abyss of poverty and his aspirations,
representative of the basic conflict between the prose and poetry of
existence that Forster aims to reconcile through perhaps Margaret in
particular. Leonard's subjection to the material problems of life is
symbolised in this chapter by his preoccupation with the umbrella. This
prevents him from responding to Margaret's conversation on the way
to Wickham Place; it is not the only difficulty, however, as Leonard's
cultural isolation means that he is not used to speaking the Schlegels'
kind of language. This is exposed in very extreme terms of contradic-
tion in the following chapter as he reads Ruskin's luxuriant prose, and
is simultaneously obliged to reply to the monosyllabic Jacky. His one
escapade, when he pursues 'beauty', is when he walks all night, but in
recounting it to the Schlegels he exposes his tendency to quote literature, and only once is he himself, in his honest negative to Helen's
question about the beauty of the dawn. Immediately afterwards he is
back to his earlier divided state of mind.

This conflict will soon be diminished somewhat by the pressure of
circumstances, and at Oniton Leonard explains to Helen how he has
had to abandon all ideas of self-improvement. He also shamefully
admits that his grandparents had been labourers and Forster here
places Leonard in a sociological panorama, in that gap produced by
urbanisation and rapid population growth, between the old, traditional
values of the land and the educated upper classes. Leonard is representative of his class's tendency to disown their rural origins and to ape the
culture of those who lead society. He moves beyond this mimetic trend,
and in his poverty descends to a kind of blackmail of his family in order
to survive, that is, by threatening them with the possibility of his
becoming a social disgrace through poverty. He eventually becomes
one of the unemployable.

Leonard's drifting existence is, however, governed by two positive
things: his tenderness for Jacky and his self-awareness, saving him
from 'oblivion' (Chapter XLI). A capacity for genuine feeling redeems
Leonard, and his last hours of life are dominated by Helen's quotation
on death: 'Death destroys a man: the idea of Death saves him.' A kind
of spiritual redemption through suffering directs Leonard's last
journey, and confirms this character's constant awareness of something greater than himself, his need for some ultimate interpretation of

life which was already implicit in his pursuit of culture. This is given an ironical twist by the fact that he meets his death under a falling book-case.

## Charles Wilcox

Charles Wilcox is really a gross caricature of his father; like him, he is impervious to others, obtuse, and he lacks his father's moments of kindness. His forehead reflects the same attitude to life, square and 'box-like' (Chapter III). Unlike other characters Charles will never change in the slightest way. He does not modify his aggressive manner at any moment, and at the close, after Leonard's death, he asserts his self-confidence, using his motor-car as a material support. Through-out the novel his car always appears with him, and even to the irritation of his father at times, as in Chapter XLII. The incident on the way to Oniton is perhaps one of the most memorable ones with Charles and motor-car when, as brisk organiser of the expedition, he seems in his element. The modern masculinity he stands for is well portrayed by the car, and his attachment to it is redolent of a whole epoch of rising materialism. His financial dependence however, robs him of the veneer of prosperity, and he appears as a rather miserable, egotistical creature in the only stage of the narrative to expose his inner thoughts, preoccu-pied by the financial situation of his own immediate family (Chapter XXV). In his relationship with Dolly he is an aggressive male, carrying his father's insensitivity to extremes.

In a way we can regard Charles as a counterpart to Leonard, another young man like himself, even though his role is less essential in the plot. Unlike Leonard, he never feels the attraction of universal values, hav-ing a very limited horizon. His impervious nature is quite the contrary to Leonard's open, subjective personality. The two characters never have anything to do with each other, until, ironically, towards the very end, their distinctive roles and natures are juxtaposed in the climactic scene of Leonard's death. Charles's blunt and impulsive gesture epitomises his character, whilst Leonard dies as the victim of circum-stance that he always was. It is fitting that Leonard should die facing Charles, as Charles is perhaps the best representative of that 'panic and emptiness' of modern life that Helen so feared, one of those people who never said 'I', and thus were never concerned by 'Pity and Justice' (Chapter XXVII).

## Aunt Juley

Aunt Juley supplies comedy with her idiosyncratic and chauvinistic belief in the infinite superiority of the English over other races. She is the only 'family' the young Schlegels have, and so represents family ties of affection. She sets off their youthful spirit, their lack of conventionality, with her realistic ways and conservative nature; she is an attractive character because of her comical diplomatic wiles and her loyalty and affection for her nieces. She plays a vital role in the plot as a kind of intermediary. The moments in which she appears are like interludes; they give a certain rhythmic pause in the sequence of dramatic events. Rather than have Margaret involved directly and too early with the Wilcoxes, it is Aunt Juley who carries out the liaison between Wickham Place and Howards End, and later it is the girls' stay with her that furnishes an extension of scenery for Margaret's and Henry's relationship. Also when Aunt Juley falls ill there is good reason for Helen to be called back from abroad. After this Aunt Juley fades out of the plot, the action becoming so close and tense that there is no room for her sort of intermediary role.

## Tibby

Tibby is a certain type of young man for whom Forster has little sympathy. His appearances in the novel are quite sporadic, but all, and in particular Chapter XXXIX, point to the same conclusion—that indifference such as Tibby's can eventually be harmful. Forster does suggest a psychological explanation for this attitude; Tibby, living in a house exclusively of women, his father dead, quite logically rejects his sisters' concern with personal relations, and when he gets to university is relieved to learn that the importance of individuals has been greatly 'overrated' (Chapter XXX). Like Charles, he has a cold nature and a limited horizon, and once his studies are over he does not seem ambitious or concerned about anything. Unlike the girls, culture to him is for personal advancement, as in the case of his study of Chinese grammar to be an interpreter. His relation to Beethoven's Fifth Symphony is revelatory, as he sits with the score open on his knee, listening knowledgeably with a technical ear, and not at all emotionally or philosophically. Finally, the reader associates Tibby with a form of sterility, a passive existence which may produce 'cold culture' (Chapter XXXIV). Tibby went to Oxford and not Cambridge, which was Forster's university; and perhaps Forster, by placing this rather unlikeable character in the 'other' university, is suggesting a fundamental gap in outlook between Tibby and himself. It is a rather facetious way of emphasising his lack of sympathy with the kind of person that Tibby represents.

Two features link Tibby to the Wilcoxes: he is obtuse in his own way, and also, like the Wilcox males, he gets hay fever, thus becoming part of the negative current in opposition to the fertility of the hay crop at the end of the novel.

---
## Dolly
---

Dolly presents an image of weak femininity, submerged by the Wilcox males at the discussion of the will in Chapter XI. She is beaten down by them, although making relevant remarks. Unlike Margaret she cannot defend herself at all, and she resorts to tears and baby-talk frequently. Her weakness reveals a complementary inadequacy in Charles, who has not had the courage (unlike his father) to marry an intelligent woman. Henry, indeed, confides in Margaret, saying that he could never live near Dolly if he were paid (Chapter XXIV). It is Dolly who allows Ruth's wish to be known by Margaret at the end, as if she were at last avenging herself on that all-male 'committee meeting' of some years before.

---
## Evie Wilcox
---

Evie appears very little in the novel. She serves as a link with the Schlegels for Henry, who uses her and her puppies as an excuse to go and see them (Chapter XVI). Physically, Evie is an athletic type, and she is 'handsome', not at all a silly, pretty girl like Dolly. She is self-centred, like her brother, interpreting events only as they affect her, as in the case of her father's engagement, which she resents. She disappears out of the novel with her wedding, having played the role of complementary family figure to her father, and only reappears at the very end, when she forms part of the Wilcox clan around Henry.

---
## Miss Avery
---

Miss Avery's appearances are brief, but bear a concise significance; she is not so much a character as a symbol. Her first appearance associates her with Ruth Wilcox, as she takes Margaret to be Ruth, coming down the stairs in Howards End (Chapter XXIII). She never quite loses this first identity nor her mysterious impact; in Chapter XXXIII she dramatically opens doors, showing her furniture arrangements to Margaret; in Chapter XL, while the Schlegel girls are talking together, Miss Avery is seen to go through the hedge by a gap, most symbolically, which she had opened up after Henry Wilcox had filled it in; it is she who hangs the Schlegels' sword on the wall (Chapter XXXIII), and it is she who comes out of the house carrying the sword after Leonard's death, ominously saying: 'Yes, murder's enough' (Chapter XLI). In all these incidents there is one common denominator: the impact is a visual one and the element of drama or surprise is present.

The last mention of Miss Avery associates her with the survival of the past through Helen's child, as she remarks on the ironic fact that

Leonard died unaware he was to be a father (Chapter XLIII). As a dramatic agent in the plot she brings about an active realisation of those notions of survival and tradition personified by Howards End.

## Jacky

Jacky, as we will see later, is really a caricature of a particular kind of person, portrayed with humour. Unlike Leonard she is not a sensitive character, and Forster exposes through her the misery of an uprooted weak individual with little to redeem her.

## Paul Wilcox

Paul Wilcox is a shadowy character, only enduring as a memory for Helen. He really appears at the end, apart from an even briefer appearance in Chapter III. At the end he returns obviously influenced by his stay in Africa; his attitude is summed up by the colonialist word 'piccaninnies', and his stance, scratching his arm as if against mosquitos, enhances this while expressing his nervous and aggressive manner.

## Frieda Mosebach

Frieda Mosebach requires a mention because she illuminates the Schlegels' Teutonic origins, and explains Forster's choice of such origins. The significant episode occurs in Chapter XIX, highlighting Helen's idealism and sense of the universal through Frieda's remark on the truth of emotion being the only certainty. (See Part 4: Points for Study, passage 4.)

## Crane

Crane, the chauffeur, is an unpleasant presence, in conjunction with the motor-car and especially with the doctor, Mansbridge, and the flyman in Chapters XXXV and XXXVI.

# Structure and style

## The plot

*Howards End*, stylistically, is a series of modulations alternating the 'inner' and 'outer' worlds in the texture of the prose. The plot itself is an interaction of two main currents represented by the Wilcoxes and the Schlegels. Margaret acts as a kind of catalyst, connecting the two currents first by her friendship with Ruth Wilcox and then by her marriage with Henry. Thus she realises her rather more abstract ambition of connecting the prose and poetry of life by reconciling antagonistic elements within the plot. As an active agent, and as the character who most expresses the author's own quest for some sort of balance, her presence dominates the narrative, and is inclined to overshadow the role of Helen, who nevertheless runs like a vital thread throughout.

Helen is the instigator of Margaret's later connecting action, as it is she who revives the acquaintance with the Wilcoxes by her stay with them. After this, we see comparatively little of her, apart from a few moments of fantasy and humour. While she is away in Germany the friendship between Ruth and Margaret develops. She returns for the gradual formation and then culmination of the Schlegel-Wilcox link through Henry's courtship of Margaret and their marriage. All through this she asserts her revulsion for the Wilcox attitudes, exacerbated by the sub-plot concerning Leonard. As she establishes a distance from the Wilcoxes, her sister moves closer to them. Helen is drawn into involvement in the sub-plot, and there are times when this parallel intrigue collides with the Wilcox current, beginning with the chance discussion on the Chelsea embankment but culminating most dramatically in the Oniton episode. This is really the climax of interaction between the two plots: here the seeds of Margaret's final understanding and compromise with Henry will be laid, subsequent to the discovery of Jacky's liaison with him; here Helen conceives the child who will connect past and future in Howards End. Helen has a vital role, but it is conveyed subtly within the plot, for she will be absent from the scene of action, and this is the kind of paradox that Forster enjoys, for the surprise of her pregnancy engenders the catharsis of the whole narrative.

The separate ways of Helen and Margaret meet again, as Leonard's death and his child's birth form a further climax in the interaction of the two plots, cementing them into one current. It is as if Forster, through this pattern of three groups of lives, three social classes, wished to go beyond such divisions and, through the catharsis, create a fundamental and lost unity. The return to nature in the 'sacred centre' of the hayfield vindicates Leonard's rural origins, and unites them with the spirit of Ruth Wilcox. Helen, the mother, transmits this to the future whilst Margaret as spiritual heir to Howards End ensures the stability of the central *locus vivendi**. Associated already with the move from Wickham Place, Margaret would seem to be the necessary organising spirit, and an active counterpart to the fertile subjectivity of Helen.

The action of the narrative, the interference of one level with another in the plot, are nearly always the result of coincidence—a frequent feature of Forster's plots. Some readers condemn them as extravagant and far-fetched, and the readers' credulity is perhaps tried by such

---

* *locus vivendi:* Latin phrase meaning 'dwelling-place'.

coincidences as the Wilcoxes' living opposite the Schlegels in London, Henry meeting the girls on the Chelsea embankment, Jacky being Henry's former mistress, or Leonard glimpsing Margaret and Tibby in St Paul's. Yet coincidence is a reality in everyday life, although we can argue that it occurs at a lower frequence, and does not concentrate on such a small portion of humanity! In *Howards End* these coincidences are triggers of action, and Forster relies on them for the network of his plot. Although a little unrealistic in their frequency, the coincidences are a reflection of the very real part that time and place play in the determination of individual lives. Also, in spite of this predominance of chance, Forster certainly gives a voice to the role of human will and resilience, in the person of Margaret in particular. Yet perhaps the most striking aspect, and one which critics are inclined to neglect, is the subtle way in which accident and impulse come together in Helen's role, and eventually assert themselves as source of the future in Leonard's child, uniting the diverse patterns of the whole narrative in one. Just as Margaret represents a controlling active element, so Helen is witness to that force outside human will. It is this force that Helen recognises in her own life, saying: 'Unreality and mystery begin as soon as one touches the body', and her words will continue by asserting the role that spontaneity and fate, complements to Margaret's wisdom, will play in the novel's ultimate unity: 'Heaven will work of itself' (Chapter XXIII).

## Language: pattern and rhythm

In *Howards End* Forster shows a vast range of possibilities in style, and displays multiple facets of his art as novelist. The novel's concern with distinct areas of human experience demands this diversification of style, and the opening maxim 'Only connect...' implies different levels of reality, as Forster expresses them, the 'poetry and prose' of life. Stylistically, they correspond to a variety in language. Sometimes, in dealing especially with the prosaic, Forster heightens descriptions by resorting to humorous depiction, often to the point of parody sketches, and *Howards End*, like his preceding novels, can be seen as social comedy. However, if we limited it to this interpretation we would be neglecting the spiritual dimension of the work. The two levels of reality alternate in the novel, creating a series of modulations which gradually move to a close with the drawn-out predominance of one modulation in particular, rather like a musical concerto where the main instrument asserts itself before the end. Preceding this ultimate expansion of the spiritual theme, the novel keeps shifting from one domain of experience to another, some chapters showing rapid oscillations.

An obvious example for the study of this process is Chapter V, where the Beethoven Fifth Symphony introduces an abstract dimension by which to reflect the inner world of each individual. The symphony, and art in general, continue as an underlying extensive theme contrasting with the humorous presentation of Leonard and Margaret conversing, where the very concise symbol of the umbrella summarises in burlesque fashion all the material problems of Leonard's existence. Chapter V combines two currents very precisely, the imaginative trend being linked in particular with Helen. Grandiose language conveys the majesty of the music, and Helen's interior world responds to it, and her obscure fear is embodied by the 'goblins' of 'panic and emptiness' alternating with a sense of majestic plenitude. By repeating the goblins motif at the end of the chapter, and in conjunction with Leonard's umbrella, Forster establishes a network of metaphor, expressive of the duality inherent in the social analysis of the work.

The second part of this chapter is an excellent piece of social comedy. Leonard, haunted by the umbrella, portrays a psychological conflict: culture, which he is trying to accumulate, is put into direct rivalry with the umbrella: 'Behind Monet and Debussy the umbrella persisted'; and here, through this persistence of his mundane preoccupation, like the 'steady beat of a drum', Forster makes a very neat parallel with Helen's 'panic and emptiness' felt in the drum passage of the symphony. Thus, through such precise stylistic devices weaving connections between Helen and Leonard, both characters are related to the basic theme of spiritual deprivation, conflicting in both with spiritual aspirations.

Thus Chapter V finally presents a thesis reflecting the fundamental conflict in the novel between inner and outer forces. The oscillatory movement is striking, and the modulations and interwoven relationships in the text create a kind of ebb and flow which Forster himself refers to at various stages of the novel in the allusions he makes to the movement of water, a parallel to the flux of human life, as in Margaret's reflection at the end of Chapter XV.

## Language and realism

A good example of realistic passages in *Howards End* is Chapter VI, and it is certainly the most sustained one; elsewhere realism is fragmentary. The umbrella in the preceding chapter is such a fragmentary piece of realism, preparing the reader for the tone of Chapter VI, in its extension of the prosaic in Leonard's life. This is the chapter of which I.A. Richards says: 'It is only ten pages long, but what other novelist, though taking a whole volume, has said as much on this theme or said it so clearly?' * Our concern here is with the style in which he treats this

---

* I.A. Richards, 'A passage to Forster: reflections on a novelist', *The Forum*, LXXVII, No. 6, December 1927. Reprinted in *Forster: a Collection of Critical Essays*, edited by Malcolm Bradbury, Prentice-Hall, Englewood Cliffs, N.J., 1966, p.20.

theme, and as Richards states, the novelist expresses it 'clearly'. For this clarity he relies on the technique of emphasising details of Leonard's sordid surroundings. Exemplary moments of this extreme realism are when an objective depiction combines with a sense of the absurd which, were it not so authentic, would render the theme quite comic; as in the case of Jacky's portrait, where Forster relishes in caricature.

The introduction conveys a physical pressure which will be emphasised by the confinement of Leonard's flat; as he walks under a tunnel on the way to his flat, he feels a pain and is 'conscious of the exact form of his eye sockets'. When Leonard meets Mr Cunningham, an amusing incongruity occurs if the reader juxtaposes Mr Cunningham's rather serious view of the possible demographic decline and the very realistic setting of their conversation, a densely populated suburb of London. The sociological theme of urban development and population flux repeated throughout the novel is given its most elaborate treatment here in this landscape of suburbia.

The flat itself is a sharp contrast to the house of Howards End; it has a 'makeshift note', and its decor and the life lived in it are rendered in a sort of verbal 'pointillism'* by which things around Leonard and Leonard's gestures interact within a very limited space. He cuts himself on Jacky's photograph frame, then he drinks tea which has been left on a shelf 'dark and silent'. These two adjectives, in their stark simplicity, are most expressive, contrasting with Forster's flowery language elsewhere. Perhaps the most sordidly realistic passage, and one where the emphasis on detail is so forced as to suggest the absurd, is the short paragraph describing the couple's meal. This is an impoverished monotony that Forster renders all the more convincing by using a kind of verbal microscope: 'a freckled cylinder of meat, with a little jelly at the top, and a great deal of yellow fat at the bottom'.

What a contrast is this to those long dialogues between the Schlegels where the only details of setting are of china, paintings, furniture or nature! Their cultural universe is one that Leonard, from his flat, sees as a 'narrow rich staircase' at Wickham Place, leading into an 'ample room'. It is this sense of space and weightlessness which portrays the educated ease of the Schlegels' lives, suggested too in the preceding chapter by Margaret's words that 'fluttered away' from Leonard like 'birds'. This ease is also suggested by Leonard's choice of reading Ruskin, who 'glided over the whispering lagoons'.

* pointillism: a painting technique employed by the Neo-Impressionists, which uses separate dots of pure colour instead of mixing pigments.

## Language as lyricism

The lyrical flow of language in Ruskin concluding Chapter VI is much more in keeping with Forster's predominant style in *Howards End* than the realistic detail preceding it, and he often relies on lyricism. In the evocation of Beethoven's symphony he exploits abstract and military vocabulary together to create a particular resonance, 'colour and fragrance broadcast on the field of battle' (Chapter V). Here the expansion of the music is conveyed in terms of visual space.

Landscape, too, is very lyrically handled, sometimes exaggeratedly so, at least for F.R. Leavis who considers that Forster 'lapses into . . . exaltations',* taking the concluding seascape passage of Chapter XIX as an example. Certainly, in this passage there is a very deliberate use of conventional poetical language, rather high-flown. If we turn to Forster's description of the English countryside we discover a very different lyricism, a blending of seasons and setting, a sense of intimacy and closeness to the pastoral: 'Celandines grew on its banks, lords-and-ladies and primroses in the defended hollows.' Such are the evocations of the scenery around Howards End. Of course, one of the most evident motifs of the pastoral is Ruth's wisp of hay which expands into the great crop of hay at the end. The Forsterian feeling for the paradoxical qualities in things is lyrically expressed by the solid form and dynamic evanescent movement of the wych-elm, 'strength and adventure in its roots' and, at the tips of its branches, 'bud clusters seemed to float in the air'. Forster refers to water as reflecting flux, and these passages are yet another voice for his lyricism. The sea is a metaphor developed to the full as an expression of Margaret's feelings after Ruth Wilcox's death (Chapter XII), or a metaphor for the impact of love, a tiny pebble in the sea of life (Chapter XX).

## Language as modernity

Such lyricism finds a sharp stylistic contrast in the novel by certain lively, surprising images. Some of these are often quoted, no doubt because of their original, modernist impact, somehow stylistically symbolic of the novel's epoch, an age of transition and the emergence of a new century. Perhaps the best-known example is when the countryside, source of lyricism as we have just remarked, is totally changed by the motor-car and so: 'It heaved and merged like porridge. Presently it congealed. They had arrived' (Chapter XXIII). The comparison is unexpected, and succeeds in communicating a total visual impression

* F.R. Leavis, 'E.M. Forster', *Scrutiny*, VII, No. 2, September 1938. Reprinted in *Forster: a Collection of Critical Essays*, p.42.

with immediacy. A similar effect is achieved in Margaret's visit to Ducie Street where the chairs of maroon leather make it look as if 'a motor-car had spawned' (Chapter XVIII). Again, the notion is far-fetched, and yet the components of the image hold together well, creating a vivid impact. Another image, closer to conventional, pictural design, but none the less original and effective, is that of the people at Ruth Wilcox's funeral, standing around like 'drops of ink'. A last, very humorous and more abstract one gives Forster's opinion on psychologists, for if a man leaves the complexities of his own psychology to be resolved by the specialist it is as if he left 'his dinner to be eaten by a steam-engine' (Chapter XXXIV). There is a whole tradition of the English sense of the absurd in this, as in Forster's portrait of Jacky in Chapter VI, reaching back to Dickens.

Throughout this discussion of Forster's style and the structure of his narrative, one distinctive feature comes to light. Whether it be a realistic passage, a piece of social comedy or of lyricism, the novelist is exploiting the weight of words, their potential towards conciseness, and sometimes, as in lyricism, towards poetry. This gives Forster's prose its variety, a parallel to his philosophical awareness of the duality of existence.

## Ideas

Contradictory notions run through *Howards End*, and show up Forster's fascination with the seemingly insoluble play of opposite forces in life. The main themes exposing this conflict are collectivism/individualism, poverty/wealth, culture/ignorance, soul/body, life/death, love/hate, emptiness/plenitude, spiritual deprivation/spiritual fulfilment, and so on. The overall search for unity can be summed up by the notion of reconcilement introduced by Margaret, and concerning in particular the very general, ubiquitous conflict between the material and the spiritual, referred to as the prose and poetry, or, in her personal problem with Henry, as the 'beast and the monk'. Margaret, in this aim at reconcilement, obviously voices the narrator's quest implicit in 'Only connect . . . ' Not only do both Schlegel girls represent a bridge uniting different social classes through the narrative structure, they also represent a search for unity and reciprocity between man and woman, especially Margaret, who goes about it lucidly.

Margaret's closeness to her author is demonstrated in part by her opinions on money, and on the movement for women's rights. In the Chelsea discussion society she expounds her ideas on finance, aware of her own position on an 'island', and her practical interpretation shocks the other women. Forster resented the hypocritical silence surrounding money matters, and so enjoys the bluntness with which the Schlegels envisage such matters here, and also in their interview with Leonard in Chapter XVI. It was as if Forster was revenging himself on what he was told as a little boy, 'Dear, don't talk about money, it's ugly.' * There are echoes of Bloomsbury in the Chelsea scene, and more specifically those Saturday evenings with the 'Apostles', that most exclusive 'Cambridge Conversazione Society' to which Forster was elected in 1901. Margaret is not a suffragette agitating for the vote; like Forster, she distrusts collective movements, inherently confident in the superiority of the individual: 'Doing good to humanity was useless', she thinks, daring to hope she may at least help a few people (Chapter XV). Her attitude to the education of the working classes reflects Forster's experience as lecturer for the Working Men's College in London, where he had started in 1902. Looking at Leonard when he arrives in Wickham Place in Chapter XIV she is surely expressing Forster's conclusions as to the 'vague aspirations, the mental dishonesty, the familiarity with the outsides of books'.

Margaret's reaction to Leonard here also gives a cohesive impression of Forster's adherence to the rural ascendancy of England, and his complementary fear of urbanisation, wondering as she does if it is really worth giving up the 'glory of the animal' for a 'tail-coat' and a 'couple of ideas'. D.H. Lawrence immediately springs to mind in his treatment of the sociological theme of town and country, his notion of the dyspeptic weakling, product of the middle classes. *Howards End* gives a panoramic view of the city, reaching from the 'abyss' over which hangs Leonard to the business milieu of Mr Wilcox who is for Leonard a distant 'superman' (Chapter XXVII). The Schlegels' independence from these two extremes upholds the position of the liberal intellectual, and their solid incomes as well as their distinctively German origins give them a further distance from both other sections of society. Forster avails of their cosmopolitanism to express his dislike of English reticence and the English cult of masculine dignity.

Forster's love of the English countryside, where he had started going on long walking tours during the years preceding *Howards End*, furnishes much of the lyricism in the book. Such a tour of Shropshire inspired the 'Oniton' episode, and Oniton corresponds to A.E. Housman's (1859–1936) 'Clun' in *A Shropshire Lad* (1896). Blending with the natural beauty of England are the traditional values upheld by Ruth Wilcox; she, in her closeness to nature, transmits the ancient rural wisdom and 'aristocracy' of the past. There unites with this another current, the individualist, liberal tradition as represented in Margaret. Thus the novel unites the two most beloved currents of

* E.M. Forster, *Two Cheers for Democracy*, p.68.

English life for Forster whilst discarding others. The aggressive Darwinist philosophy of the Wilcoxes receives a rude shock, and the paradox lies in the contrast between their prosperity and power, purely outer and materialistic, and their spiritual deprivation. Money, says the novel, is a purely practical necessity, and should not be gained for its own sake, but for the furtherance of the rather more intangible realities of the spirit. In fact, a parallel between the financial and spiritual themes is implied by the phrasing of that moment of final understanding between Margaret and Helen, 'the inner life had paid'. These words are a triumphant vindication of the Schlegels' belief in the personal forces, an affirmation of their predominance over the outer, impersonal forces.

## Language and ideas

Forster's acute sense of the multiple possibilities of language is not merely part of a stylistic technique. Language is also a subject that Forster considers in itself, in relation to other ideas in the text. The problem of language and culture is posed by the juxtaposition between Margaret's easy flow of words, like 'birds' in Chapter V, and, in the next chapter, Jacky, for whom the 'spoken word was rare'. The final exchange between herself and Leonard towards the end of this chapter exposes her lack of receptivity to language also, by her 'degraded deafness'. Leonard's miserable situation is related closely to the fundamental reality of language, caught as he is between such 'conversation' with Jacky and his reading of Ruskin. His incommunicability in educated circles is cruelly emphasised by his expressive 'No' in reply to Helen about the dawn, and otherwise his language is hopelessly second-hand, springing from his reading and not from within himself.

It is Helen who explains this essential link between language and self that Forster sees as one of the most determining factors in the individual; she speaks of two kinds of people, those who live 'straight from the middle of their heads' and those who, on the other hand, 'can't say "I"'. Leonard may not be armed by education with the linguistic means of expression, but he at least remains self-aware even in the depths of misery, saved from 'muddledom' by his capacity to say 'I' (Chapter XLI). However, the whole class he belongs to is threatened with incommunicability, and there is a modern, prophetic ring about Forster's opening to Chapter VI, where this observation relates well to the conclusion on Jacky's poverty of language and her 'deafness'. Leonard is seen by Forster to be on the verge of an abyss 'where nothing counts, and the statements of Democracy are inaudible'.

Complementary to this 'inaudible' situation of the lower classes is Forster's view of language within urban civilisation: Margaret, in

London, notices the 'language of hurry'—'clipped words, formless sentences, potted expressions of approval or disgust' (Chapter XIII), a vision proleptic of T.S. Eliot's Waste Land. In an intermediate position is the rich, uneducated millionaire, the rising opportunistic builder of the new city, who will erect flats in place of the Schlegels' home in London. Margaret found him 'not a fool' on hearing him discuss Socialism, but her conclusion implies the irresponsibility of this city figure, manipulating the nomadic population through an acquired language, for 'true insight began just where his intelligence ended' (Chapter XIII).

Another acquired language, that which Leonard lacks, is the intellectual jargon of the Schlegels' circle, and at the luncheon party two languages come into play, Ruth Wilcox's and that of Margaret and her friends. Like Leonard, Ruth does not speak the right language, but he has been exiled from his origins for ever by urban democracy, whereas she is only exiled temporarily from her world at Howards End by her stay in London. She belongs to a totally different region of experience, so at home with nature that she is part of it. Margaret, as Ruth takes her leave, suddenly senses this, and realises that the language of her circle is meaningless; they are like 'gibbering monkeys' (Chapter IX).

Thus language is not only in the narrative as an expression of the characters' diversity, it is also commented upon and integrated by Forster within a whole social panorama, and exposed as a vital and fundamental element of human existence. It is perhaps in his idea of language as portrayed in *Howards End* that we find one of the main sources of the novel's modernity and relevance today.

# Part 4

# Hints for study

HERE ARE A FEW WORDS of guidance to help you in studying *Howards End*:

*(1) First reading:*
A quick preliminary reading should give you an impression of the work as a whole, and allow you simply to enjoy it as a story. During this first reading you can already note down at random anything that strikes you as interesting, original or surprising; in re-reading these few notes afterwards you will recognise individual stylistic traits running through the text, and thus before actually studying the novel you will have developed a feeling of the author's style and approach.

*(2) Second reading:*
This is a more careful and applied reading where you must break the work down into distinctive episodes. Notice how the plot develops and divides, as, for example, in the arrival of Leonard; note also how the intricacies of the plot hold together within the structure of the whole, and how the final outcome emerges from the narrative. Study the ideas and their presentation through: (a) characters, (b) symbols, (c) language, (d) narrative structure, and see how far the narrator himself intrudes.

Study the setting within which the action takes place, both the sociological/historical backgrounds, the physical surroundings and landscape, and notice how and where these various aspects come together.

*(3) After the second reading:*
You should now be very familiar with the novel both as interacting parts and a cohesive unit, and when answering questions or writing essays do not forget these two complementary features. Avoid:

(*a*) a fragmentary discussion of characters without relating them to the underlying ideas.

(*b*) simply retelling the story without any consideration of the questions asked. (Remember, the examiner is already familiar with the story!)

(c) a too abstract discussion of the ideas with little or no reference to their realisation within the narrative.

Now you must select points in the novel to help you to develop your knowledge of the plot and style; this is most important, as it will give you references and examples immediately available in your mind when you come to essay writing. Some of these points have been selected for you, with notes to show the kind of rapid analysis required, that can best bring you to grips with the text itself.

## Points for study

Discuss the imagery and thematic relevance of the following passages:

(1) The description of Wickham Place towards the beginning of Chapter II, from 'She broke off...' to '...the precious soil of London'.
*Notice the following:* the vertical parallel in growth of population/ buildings; recurrent stylistic motif of the sea, here to convey urban flux, and within that flux the isolation of the Schlegels, that is, 'estuary' and also 'backwater' (used in the same sense in the passage in Chapter XVII describing Margaret's arrival at Simpson's; see pp. 63–4 below); 'profound', 'cavernous', 'promontory'; ultimate reality of finance underlying precious soil, a basic theme in the novel.

(2) The passage describing Charles's drive through Hilton in Chapter III, from 'They drew up...' to '...was his comment'.
*Notice the following:* Charles's imperviousness: he does not reply to Aunt Juley, then makes a comment quite irrelevant to her conversation; the 'invasion' of the countryside by the motor-car as seen in the 'dust' image, and the modern resonance of the verb 'percolated' associated with this; irony of the word 'wisdom' in Charles's remark if we juxtapose it with the narrator's appreciation of Ruth Wilcox later at the end of the same chapter: 'that instinctive wisdom...'.

(3) There is a significant psychological evocation of Margaret, from 'Her mind darted...' to '...has been wiped away', just before her letter to Mrs Wilcox in Chapter VIII.
*Notice the following:* a succinct summary of Margaret's lucidity and objectivity: in contrast to Helen's impulsive nature or Henry's obtuse practicality, she represents an ideal balance; the military metaphor to express the exercise of the conscious faculties over the subconscious; the quotation from *Hamlet*, rejecting excessive subjectivity and romanticism in its juxtaposition with Margaret's humanistic use of reason.

(4) The above extract, emblematic of Forster's quest for balance, can be seen as complementary to another facet of the Schlegels' personalities, their Germanic sense of the universal in the passage between Helen and Frieda in Chapter XIX, from 'One is certain...' to '...the pretty, the adequate'.
*Notice the following:* an explanation of Forster's having chosen Teutonic origins for the Schlegels, thus widening the scope of the novel

beyond what he considers to be the limits of the English mind, elucidated here in contrasting terms; Frieda's minor role as an ideal support to Helen's adherence to the abstract, the subconscious.

(5) There is a paragraph in Chapter XXXI evoking Margaret and Henry in their marital relations, from 'His affection . . . ' to ' . . . touch his peace'.
*Notice the following:* the humorous standpoint chosen, as Forster takes a sideways glance, from the husband's point of view; male condescension in Henry's interpretation of Margaret's behaviour, springing from 'nerves'; Forster's use of dramatic irony if such a passage is apposed to Henry's eventual weakness of character; the satirical exploitation of the conventional image of man and woman as 'warrior' and 'recreation'; the biblical, pompous tone of the concluding words.

(6) There is another very striking piece of psychological observation, already mentioned in Part 3 of these Notes, that concerns Helen's experience with Paul. It appears in Chapter XXXIV, from 'The more Margaret . . . ' to ' . . . one cannot say', the length of two paragraphs.
*Notice the following:* Forster's extended development of the 'seed' metaphor as a reflection of contemporary theories on the importance of the unconscious forces in directing human reactions; the emphasis on sexual frustrations as a source of psychological problems; the suggestion of future trouble for Helen, thus a proleptic passage in the narrative structure.

(7) The opening passage in Chapter XXVI from 'Next morning . . . ' to ' . . . upper reaches'.
*Notice the following:* the movement of light and shadow, and animated detail of the cat; perspective: close solidity emerging from mist into light/the river appearing, striking the eye and drawing it to the limit of the horizon; biographical and literary associations: Forster's walking tour of Shropshire (1907) and his attachment to A.E. Housman's *A Shropshire Lad*. Oniton was Housman's 'Clun'. Compare this landscape to others in the book, that is Hertfordshire, and the Swanage coastline.

## Specimen questions

(1) Discuss the narrator's interventions in the novel; what do they contribute?

(2) Referring back to the motif of the sea discussed in Part 3 above, choose other examples of this image and analyse them stylistically.

(3) Discuss the language Forster uses in his caricature of Jacky in Chapter VI. Who are the ancestors of his parody in English literature?

(4) 'I have no mystic faith in the people. I have in the individual. He seems to me a divine achievement and I mistrust any view which belittles him.' Discuss this in relation to *Howards End*.

(5) Referring back to the character sketches in Part 3 of these Notes, discuss:

> (a) Margaret, and her attitude to money, in further detail.
> (b) the Wilcox men, comparing them at various stages of the narrative.
> (c) Tibby's reactions in the episodes involving him.
> (d) Leonard's evolution and last days.

(6) Take the 'proverbial' remark: 'It is the starving imagination and not the well-nourished that is afraid' (Chapter XXIII), and discuss its relevance to the novel and its universal truth. Then select other such remarks in the novel, and analyse them in the same way.

(7) Write on death in *Howards End*, that is, on the idea of death and how it figures in the plot.

(8) Discuss Nature and civilisation in *Howards End*.

(9) Describe how Forster brings conflicting values into play.

(10) Study the dialogue of each major character and show how it expresses their individual traits.

## Specimen questions and guideline answers

The next questions are followed by analysis of the text or essay projects. Before you read them, study each question for yourself and then compare your ideas with our suggestions.

(1) Read the passage describing Margaret's arrival at Simpson's restaurant in Chapter XVII, from 'But when she saw Evie . . .' to ' . . . her feeling of loneliness vanished'. Then answer the four questions below.

(a) *Discuss how the language situates the characters in relation to each other, and to the setting.*
The first paragraph opens with Evie as an obviously strong presence, menacingly placed at the entrance to the restaurant, 'staring fiercely'. Adjectives and adverbs here evoke the impression she makes on Margaret: the nouns referring to simple, concrete things are qualified by more elaborate adjectives evocative of Evie's rather unfeminine character—she belongs to a certain class of 'athletic' women, her voice is 'gruffer' and her manner more 'downright' than before. The paragraph moves from this physical image of Evie to conclude with Margaret's inner thoughts. As the 'foolish virgin' she experiences a sense of

inferiority, and this is translated into an abstract concept on quite another linguistic level to the first part: she feels 'isolation' and her situation is emblematic of a whole social context. This is summarised cohesively in a metaphor as she senses the 'vessel of life slipping past her'.

Margaret's isolation here as an independent woman having problems about houses and furniture will extend and develop into a sociological isolation in the following paragraph. We see Forster's constant preoccupation with Margaret's standpoint, juxtaposed to those of others (and here it happens to be Evie). This obvious concern with Margaret grows with the use of abstract nouns: virtue, wisdom, conviction, futility, backwater of art and literature, surprise, loneliness.

The physical surroundings in the second paragraph elaborate on that suggestion of menace already in Evie's stance in the first paragraph. The author uses few words, and in the evocation is succinct. There are two stages which emphasise Margaret's subjective feelings, and they correspond to a concrete, physical description of the place. Here psychology and movement within a particular setting interact. Margaret 'trod the staircase' and it is 'narrow', leading her into the dining-room, which is realistically, and emphatically, called the 'eating-room'. She is not only confronted with the visual scene of the restaurant, but also by her own sudden impression of futility. Thus the simple architectural features of her entrance are exploited to convey a progressive metaphysical sensation.

In exposing the juxtaposition of both characters within a given area, in this case a restaurant, Forster has made very neat use of stance and of setting. You could almost draw a diagram emphasising this juxtaposition: Evie, a dominant presence, staring aggressively into the space before her; Margaret, on the contrary, passively receiving the full impact of *angst*\* simultaneously with the visual impact of the scene before her. The stylistic presentation of this contrast is deceptively simple, yet conveys intangible psychological realities: Evie, impervious, looking outwards at the world, Margaret, subjective, invaded by a sense of inadequacy.

### (b) How do the two characters emerge from the text?

As we have seen through the above stylistic remarks, the two characters are diametrically opposed. Evie's gaze is an aggressive, unthinking one, reflecting the Wilcox insensitivity; she is physically active, athletic, and she is very sure of herself. She seems to have adopted a definitive attitude to Margaret, which will not change, whereas Margaret, a more receptive person, whose attitudes are much less rigid, is evidently more affected by what happens around her.

\* *angst*: German word meaning 'anxiety' and used to denote a sensation of malaise and alienation.

(c) *What does the author say here about social classes?*
Evie, as a representative of the Wilcox clan, shares the men's obtuseness, portrayed, as we have just seen, by her stance before the world. Her athletic aspect is redolent of a certain physical strength, wealth and activity which contrast with Margaret as a member of the liberal, intellectual class. Forster points out the different sociological rhythms, how the rising wealthy industrial class seems to be encroaching on and bypassing the intellectual leisured class. In the biographical introduction in Part I, the origins of this attitude were suggested; it was prevalent among young intellectuals growing up surrounded by materialistic attitudes of a new upper class based on wealth acquired overnight. Margaret's feeling of helplessness, her uprootedness over houses and furniture, her sensation of being left behind by events, convey the conflict between her class and Evie's. The isolation of her class is emphasised by the word 'backwater'; she is far from the busy flow of city life and finance that is governed by the moneyed families like the Wilcoxes.

Forster does not neglect to make a comment on the clergy, a class he did not appreciate. The image of the clergyman waiting for a copious lunch is a rather traditional negative one! Note the sketch of that other profession he disliked, in Dr Mansbridge later on in the novel.

(d) *Is there any suggestion of the plot's future development?*
Apart from the ideas on the social classes which emerge from this passage—a fundamental theme in *Howards End*—there is a stimulating suggestion with regard to the plot. Margaret's feelings are especially strong because of the social gap between herself and Evie, but there is also a feminine conflict between them. Evie's blooming physique and her engagement are felt by Margaret as a slight on her own lack of attraction and sentimental involvement. She belongs to a circle where people never 'got married' or 'succeeded in remaining engaged'; therefore her pleasure at seeing Henry Wilcox arrive anticipates her future acceptance, and these preceding remarks explain her marriage to Henry partly as a gesture of loneliness and isolation from male society.

---

(2) Referring back to 'Language: pattern and rhythm' in Part 3 of these Notes, describe the alternation in theme and style in Chapter XI.

---

After the abrupt and simple statement about Mrs Wilcox's funeral, death is portrayed in the traditional imagery of space and silence, in the landscape and the cemetery, but a contrasting motif running through this account maintains the Forsterian obsession with the inherent duality of existence.

The woodcutter, in his youth and vigour, represents life and love, and reaches back to idyllic pastoral days; he provides a complementary motif to Tom, the young boy playing in the straw. The grave is framed in this pastoral theme: taking one of the chrysanthemums Margaret had left for the grave, the woodcutter leaves to find his love, and the scene becomes one of 'silence absolute'. Forster then elaborates in rather majestic prose on the nocturnal winter sky over church and cemetery, in pictural language of romantic graveyard scenes; this passage then closes with the woodcutter's return after a night of 'joy'. There is a link between him and Mrs Wilcox, a vital, living one in the flowers, and the woodcutter regrets not having taken them all.

This short paragraph forming a cohesive poetical unit presents love and death in immediate contrast; death with all it implies of the infinite as a steady centre to the departure and return, the ebb and flow of the woodcutter's night. The reality of death here contrasts with and also complements the abstract notion of death as a constant presence within life. Helen states this resonance of death in her words to Leonard in Chapter XXVII. Ruth Wilcox's death is witness to Helen's statement as her death does not diminish the influence of the values she perpetuates, and in quixotic fashion she survives through her will. Flowers, the counterpart of death, associated with the vitality of the woodcutter's love, are also associated with Ruth Wilcox earlier in the novel. Margaret, as the donor of the flowers, as Ruth's friend and spiritual heir, is part of the vital link; significantly at the end of the chapter this link establishes itself as a current outside the Wilcox clan. Evie resents the chrysanthemums, and Henry defends the gesture on the grounds of Margaret's German origins, thus expressing his relative openness which will lead him to marriage, and make him part of the current exterior to his family.

Through the detail of the chrysanthemums a connection has been made between the opening and close of the chapter, a detail parallel to the deep, vital bond between Mrs Wilcox and Margaret which will gather momentum as Margaret begins to know Howards End and finally Mrs Wilcox's wish is granted. Although not as emblematic as the umbrella motif in Chapter V, the chrysanthemums, even if they only arise out of casual conversation, do not recur by chance at the end of the chapter; like the umbrella, this detail, too, forms part of the complex pattern of dual themes within the space of the chapter, and, much as in poetic structure, it is part of those semantic elements that support the antagonism which is central to the novel's argument.

This 'poem' however, would be incomplete without the social comedy, and in this chapter the second part, as in Chapter V, is a humorous presentation of human psychology. Unlike the earlier example it is not a study of the mind of one of the protagonists, but rather a social satire of a group of people witnessed by a 'commentator'. Forster humorously portrays the family's astounded reaction to Ruth Wilcox's will, and the consequent 'committee meeting' is one of the best examples in the novel of his satirical style. The women are the decor in this meeting between the two males, and Henry and Charles are shown as dominant figures whose sentiments are mutual.

One long paragraph summarises the atmosphere, opening with the marginal role of the women, whose presence is merely physical, contributing nothing to the debate in hand. Dolly is weeping, having been silenced by her husband, and Evie is scowling like an angry boy, which shows up her mute masculinity. The satire's main focus is on the business-like attitude of the men to what is basically a spiritual matter, and they do not concern themselves with the emotional side of the affair, not stopping to ask themselves a single question. Light and sound both frame this gathering and Forster exploits them stylistically as a suitable background. The light is hard and white, the sun is totally unnoticed, and so time is only seen in terms of the business in hand: 'the clock struck ten with a rich and confident note'.

It is now that the narrator himself intervenes, and his comments are ironical. He begins by justifying the Wilcox attitude, but as he does so he confirms an opposite opinion, and so, as in the more poetical passages we have just discussed, the author's intention is based on an inherent duplicity. He starts by saying that there was no reason why Howards End should be handed over to Margaret, deciding that the written request was too 'flimsy'. He then moves on to demonstrate the spiritual depth behind this request, a depth totally ignored by the Wilcoxes, whom he does not blame, but yet condemns by the sarcasm of his conclusion. Their action of throwing the note in the fire was 'natural' and 'fitting'. Exploiting this irony to the full, he then openly denounces their indifference to what was fundamentally a 'personal appeal'. Thus the appeal that was too 'flimsy' at the beginning of the passage is totally vindicated and even shown to be the contrary. It is completely validated by the fact of being personal, thus belonging to a radically different set of values than the Wilcoxes' impersonal standards of judgement.

Thus the chapter closes on the narrator's own justification of Ruth Wilcox, and rejoins the meditation on her death; this is cleverly paralleled by the repeated image of the chrysanthemums, a typically Forsterian emblem knitting together so many contrasting elements in the modulations of his prose.

---

(3) Discuss the theme of love in *Howards End*.

---

As you have seen from the character sketches in Part 3 of these Notes, each character presents different facets of human nature, and a fundamental difference is to be found in their various ways of responding to each other. It is through them, and through their involvements in the plot, that Forster exposes some of his most basic concepts concerning love.

The Schlegel sisters are perhaps the most individual expression of these concepts in that they go beyond the more conventional attitudes of the other characters. Their idealistic natures, especially Helen's, bring them to grips with the personal, inner world, which is upheld throughout the novel and strongly contrasted with the somewhat unemotional world of the Wilcoxes, where Dolly and Charles live a rather conventional marriage or Henry the conventional combination of adulterous moments and a socially respectable marriage.

The fact that the Schlegels live in their 'backwater', their intellectual and cultural circle, already sets them apart, and exposes them to different possibilities of experience. Henry Wilcox, when they are entertaining Leonard, comments on their rather individual ways with people, and even sees them as needing his paternalistic protection. In a way, when the narrative reveals the culmination of their curiosity with regard to Leonard in Helen's pregnancy the reader (and there were many such reactions to the book in 1910) could be conventional and agree with Henry. However, Forster is there to say that love is not what Henry Wilcox or convention may consider it to be, and that Helen's pregnancy is a consequence of spontaneity and warmth of feeling; also, it is a consequence of Henry's repression of his son, if we are to consider Forster's remarks on the pressure of denied instinct, and how this repression can influence and even determine the behaviour of an individual throughout his or her life. The following words are closer to Helen than Margaret: 'Life is indeed dangerous, but not in the way morality would have us believe. It is indeed unmanageable . . . because it is a romance, and its essence is romantic beauty' (Chapter XII). In relation to this statement Margaret is a figure of self-sacrifice; she is the loving guardian of the perennial values Ruth Wilcox stood for earlier. Both she and Helen do realise love but in totally different ways. Helen fulfils her first sexual awakening by becoming a mother, but rejects men; Margaret too, has a very particular approach in that she acknowledges in a strikingly lucid fashion that her marriage is a compromise, and she loses the one aspect that really drew her to Henry when he no longer has that veneer of masculinity she saw through but enjoyed. On the contrary, she eventually finds herself in an almost maternal, dominant position before a weak husband.

At the end of the novel, as Helen rejects men, Margaret rejects children for herself, concluding that it takes all types to make a world. Despite her aphoristic wisdom here, we cannot ignore the fact that neither of them comes to a true fulfilment of sexual love, and it is as if Forster the realist were pointing out the shortcomings of human beings before the promises of youth. This statement is, none the less, made in a background of spiritual realities embodied by Howards End and the field's 'sacred centre', and, above all, as Margaret and Helen talk in this final scene, we cannot forget the love that unites them, 'rooted in common things' and the source of their survival. It is perhaps this 'inner life' shared by the two girls, and that had 'paid', which is really the most individual and unique declaration of love in the whole novel.

# Part 5

# Suggestions for further reading

## The text

FORSTER, E.M.: *Howards End*, Edward Arnold, London, 1910, etc., (Abinger Edition) 1973; Penguin Books, Harmondsworth, 1941, etc.; latest reprint, 1981.

## Biography

FURBANK, P.N.: *E.M. Forster: a Life*, 2 vols, Secker & Warburg, London, 1978.

KING, FRANCIS: *E.M. Forster and his World*, Thames & Hudson, London, 1978.

## Criticism

ARMSTRONG, PAUL B.: 'E.M. Forster's *Howards End* : the existential crisis of the liberal imagination', *Mosaic*, 8, 1974.

BEER, J.B.: *The Achievement of E.M. Forster*, Chatto & Windus, London, 1962.

BRADBURY, MALCOLM (ED.): *Forster: a Collection of Critical Essays*, Prentice-Hall, Englewood Cliffs, N.J., 1966.

GARDNER, PHILIP: *E.M. Forster*, 'Writers and Their Work' series, Longman, Harlow, 1977.

GRANSDEN, K.W.: *E.M. Forster*, 'Writers and Critics' series, Oliver & Boyd, Edinburgh, 1962.

HARDY, JOHN EDWARD: '*Howards End* : the sacred center', *Man in the Modern Novel*, University of Washington Press, Washington, 1964.

MCCONKEY, JAMES: *The Novels of E.M. Forster*, Cornell University Press, New York, 1957.

STALLYBRASS, OLIVER (ED.): *Aspects of E.M. Forster*, Edward Arnold, London, 1969.

TRILLING, LIONEL: *E.M. Forster*, Hogarth Press, London, 1951.

WARNER, REX: *E.M. Forster*, 'Writers and Their Work' series, Longman, London 1950.

# The author of these notes

CAROLINE MACDONOGH was educated at Trinity College, Dublin and the Sorbonne, Paris. She teaches English language and literature at the University of Caen in Normandy, France, where she collaborates with the University department of Irish studies in their research and publications. She has published numerous articles on her father, the Anglo-Irish poet Patrick MacDonogh, and is completing a study of his work.

# The first 200 titles